THE DISINFORMER

Peter Ustinov
THE DISINFORMER

Two novellas

Doubleday Canada Limited
Toronto

Published in Canada by
Doubleday Canada Limited,
105 Bond Street, Toronto,
Ontario, M5B 1Y3

By arrangement with
Michael O'Mara Books Limited, London

Canadian Cataloguing in Publication Data

Ustinov, Peter
The disinformer

ISBN 0-385-25224-2

1. Title

PR6041.S73D58 1989   823'.914   C89-093838-5

Typeset by DP Photosetting,
Aylesbury, Bucks
Printed and bound in Great Britain by
Billings, Worcester

POUR HÉLÈNE

aimée et amie

CONTENTS

The Disinformer

A Nose By Any Other Name

The Disinformer

His name hardly matters; he used so many. But like
most people, he was eager for one name to be more
important than the others, like roots, which seem
such a necessary anchor in life. He had written his
memoirs, but they were still in manuscript, and he
had not even submitted them to the competent
authorities, since, as he claimed, there was no
authority competent to pronounce a judgment, or
even to exercise censorship over a book of his. So
why go through the hassle? It would be time enough
after his death for the copies to be discovered, one in
his desk, the other in a bank-vault, and then all hell
would doubtless break loose. He smiled occasionally
at the prospect, although he recognized a little sadly
that he would not be there to enjoy the chaos he
wished to create.

The name typed on the cover of the manuscript
was Hilary Glasp, which sounds false enough to be
genuine. His father, Mervyn Glasp, had been an
official of the Syrian Railways, and Hilary had been
born inadvertently and prematurely in a crowded

station waiting room somewhere on the Beirut–
Damascus line, and his mother had died of
embarrassment shortly after. Brought up by nurses
and babysitters, the boy had spoken Arabic with
greater facility than English until he was sent to an
English preparatory school at the usual age of eight.
He was not a particularly brilliant pupil either there
or in his public school, but his ability to speak fluent
Arabic gave him a kind of exclusivity, and later on,
during the war years, it became invaluable.

'Awabic? That's unusual, isn't it?' the Personnel
Selection office had exclaimed, incredulous.

'Not for me,' Hilary had replied, with that mixture
of demureness and arrogance which had marked his
years in MI5, jockeying unceasingly for position
while seeming to be half asleep. After the unpleasant
rigours of basic training, he was sent to a refresher
course in colloquial Arabic, where he spent most of
the time correcting the syntax and grammar of his
teacher, at first tactfully, soon blatantly. Those who
are too clever attract the suspicion of their superiors,
but Hilary's talent for seeming to hold a great deal
back quickly convinced the intelligence establishment that he was a man worthy of confidence, who
did not brandish his abilities, but rather used them as
a safe-deposit.

His war was largely spent in the Middle East,
leaning on bars in Cairo, interrogating delinquents
in Palestine, generally doing the necessary to create
an impression of unhurried and resourceful resil-
ience. He did not run many risks; he would not have

liked that, but he created many useful contacts with shady characters which were to stand him in good stead as the swell of seniority carried him upwards in the hierarchy.

After the war, the Middle East remained his bailiwick, and most of his time, up to his retirement, was taken up between London and Beirut. He preferred the latter, because there he was his own master, able to dispose of his leisure as he wished, and quite free to neglect the frontier between that leisure and work. Away from the surveillance of headquarters, he could easily sit in cafés sipping arak while watching nothing in particular, and he could spend his evenings in squalid night-clubs on the pretext that he had contacts there. By comparison, London was a hotbed of jealousy, backbiting, and mistrust. He liked absolutely no one, and found Levantine chicanery much easier to live with than the constipated decency and ill grace of head office. That is, until his retirement.

Some of his colleagues had emigrated when their time was up, to Kenya, Florida or Australia. One of them, with alacrity, had written an autobiography, therefore attracting the wrathful indignation of the British Government, who responded with a cascade of legal actions, none of which were in any way effective except in that they gave invaluable publicity to the offending volume, and made it seem necessary reading to all those interested in the times we live in, which it was not. It also managed to queer the pitch for all the other old spies who sat in their minimal enclaves in Mombasa, the Algarve, or wherever, with their books half-finished and destined to remain that way. Hilary had actually finished his, naming names and spraying it with acid as a gardener will spray his plants with pesticide. Occasionally, in the evening, or during nights of insomnia, he would re-read portions of it, altering a line here and there to make it more pointed, or less ambivalent. Then he would fall into an untroubled slumber with a thin smile on his lips.

Retirement is always a time of challenge for those who estimate that it has come too early, and Hilary, who had conducted much of his active life as though he had retired prematurely, now began to become tense and fidgety when the torpor he had always cultivated was imposed upon him.

Occasionally he would unearth old address books from battered attaché cases, documents he had used in writing his memoirs, and go through them, name by name, as a kind of inventory of ill-repute, of creatures who only came to their own in the half-light.

The names not only evoked moments of irritation, hilarity, or even of mystery, but they seemed now to be litanies to lost opportunity. Hilary felt at times like a tennis player who had peaked too early in history, when men still wore the colours of club or nation with pride and altruism. There was all that absurd talk of letting the side down, or playing with a straight bat. Espionage had been practised according to the same rigid rules. Not only had it been necessary to conduct one's affairs with decency, but one had expected this requisite decency in others. Then, with the onslaught of consumerism, and its attendant venality, a spy had rapidly become a free-lance professional, operating in an open market, one ear to the ground, the other receptive to the highest bidder. And this corruption applied not only to individuals, but to entire organizations, who were given to processes entitled variously disinformation and destabilization, and therefore on occasions were on intimate terms with their sworn enemies in the growing market for the sale and purchase of infor-mation, a seedy stock exchange in which every valid tit-bit, every nuance of treachery vacillated in worth according to the tide of the moment. How rich Hilary could have been had he been born twenty, even ten years later!

Now he was relegated to being a fossil, a last bitter remnant of that tragic generation of spies who lived on salary and pension instead of making themselves into corporations with post-office boxes in the Cayman Islands, in opulent anonymity. The memoirs were but a backlash of this feeling of betrayal by a society which had evolved too late in history for the creature comforts of those who had lived by rules and regulations, but who had survived long enough to see younger men prosper in forbid-den fields.

And curiously enough, this inner rage made Hilary and his like extremely vain about the lower-ing of standards. They spoke with acerbity about professionalism, and the cold comforts of the non-profit-making past, while deriding the carelessness of the new-fangled lot who couldn't keep a secret if able to sell it. They were both sarcastic about modern spies and furiously jealous of them.

It was in this strange mood that Hilary sat down one evening to watch the nine o'clock news on television. He had not been sleeping well, waking up in the night with a sudden anguish, or an involuntarily nervous reaction of an arm or leg. He imagined that the cadence of his breathing was sometimes broken, and he had difficulty in forgetting about it, and leaving his heart to its own patient devices. He could only guess that these were symptoms of all-enveloping age, but it also seemed as though his body were expressing some deep-rooted dissatisfaction at his mode of life. Perhaps retirement, the daily inactivity feeding off the cerebrality of his existence, the lack of focus and of aim, were all contributing to this contained hysteria, these tiny yet disturbing explosions in the quiet of the night.

The nine o'clock news began. The Prime Minister had made a speech somewhere in the north, while opening a crèche in which working mothers could leave their children during the day. Those running the crèche were the recently unemployed, trained to this new duty in a two weeks' crash course. A junior minister had indiscreetly revealed plans for a 'partial privatization' of the Royal Navy, which provoked hostile reactions from a group of admirals on the verge of retirement, but extracted a rather more positive reaction from a celebrated biscuit company which declared itself willing to 'adopt' a frigate for a start, on condition the name of the ship was changed to reflect the glory of its benefactor. The Prime Minister again, earlier in the day, said, while receiving an honorary degree, that the country must return to the values of the first Elizabethan age, now that Victorian values had been achieved. She also reiterated, in answer to an unprincipled heckler, that 'You can't buck the market.' A Minister of the Crown alleged that the broadcasting media had a 'very perceptible bias leftwards'. There were many more mustard gas victims in an obscure internecine conflict on the Euphrates than was generally supposed. A rampaging Vietnam veteran had shot fifteen people in a supermarket in Terre Haute, Indiana, after having seen 'Rampage', an Oscar-winning film on the same subject.

Hilary was watching all this with his sardonic mask in place, reflecting on the absurdity of it all, linked with his utter impotence in the face of this nightly maelstrom of debris from the world's digestive tract. The events of the day were described with the portentous morosity by which an award-winning newscaster is recognized as such. Suddenly the newscaster hesitated, and said, as though making a fresh start,

'This, just in from West Kensington, London. A car parked outside a shop selling Irish knitwear exploded this afternoon. Two passers-by, believed to be Jamaican, were hurt, one of them seriously.

Neither the responsibility nor the motive for the crime has yet been established, although it is not unreasonable to suppose that the IRA are the instigators of the crime, in the light of the nature of the shop the bomb was presumably intended to destroy.'

Just like the police to jump to such obvious conclusions. The way of thinking reminded Hilary of so much that he had had to suffer in London after the war. Why should the IRA blow up a shop trading in Irish jumpers and cardigans? Were the targets suddenly so minimal at a time when they were known to have sophisticated weapons which could almost be described as artillery?

On a sudden impulse, Hilary dialled the number of a leading London tabloid, and asked to speak to the night editor. He gave his name as Abdul Farhaz, and spoke in Arabic to imaginary people in the room while awaiting the night editor, so that when the latter came on the line he would first be treated to some relaxed Arabic banter.

'Harry Putner, night editor.'

'Ah. The bomb which exploded today in London.'

'Yes?'

'It was our work.'

'Who are you?'

'A brother of the Martyrs of the Seventeenth of September.'

'Where are you speaking from?'

'Beirut.'

'Beirut? Give me your name again –'

'No.'

And Hilary hung up. All he had to do now was to wait. He had been sparing with the needle; now it had to be seen if the serum had taken.

He slept well that night, as though part of his mind had acquired a measure of serenity. At the first light he made himself a strong cup of tea as usual. Russian Caravan mixture. Then he settled to watch the breakfast programme on television. 'But first, the news,' said the jolly girl, indecently radiant for the hour of the morning. The newscaster appeared, and immediately took up the strings from the night before.

'Yesterday's bomb outrage in West Kensington, London, has been attributed by an anonymous caller to an organization describing itself as the Martyrs of the Seventeenth of September. This is the first time this organization, believed to be Palestinian, has been in evidence, although Scotland Yard last night would not rule out a hoax. Just a half an hour ago, fuel was added to the mystery by a second anonymous phone call, claiming that the organization responsible for the attempt was the Brotherhood of the Crescent Moon, believed to be an offshoot of the faction led by Abu Nidal in Damascus. It was at first thought that the target was the Bit O'Blarney knitwear shop, but it has now been established that the red Reliant Kitten car was registered in the name of Jaffar Bin Aziz, the brother of the Deputy Mayor of Gaza, claimed to be a collaborator with the Israeli authorities by the militant wing of the PLO. A

spokesman for the IRA poured scorn on the sugges-
tion that that organization had anything to do with
it. In the words of Seamus O'Tumelty, one of the
leaders of the military section, 'What would we be
doing blowing up an Irish business making an honest
living when there's so many British targets doing the
opposite?'

Hilary looked at his watch. Then he called Beirut.
He spoke in Arabic.

'Is Ahmed Kress there?'

He waited a moment. His face expressed nothing.
Then a slight smile broke on his lips, the nearest
approximation to charm of which he was capable.

'Ahmed Kress?' ... Guess ... No ... No ... I am not
Arabic ... Hilary Glasp.'

There was much effusiveness from far away.
After joining in the pleasantries, Hilary became
more serious, 'No, I must admit, it was not just to
renew old acquaintances – Who are the Brotherhood
of the Crescent Moon? ... You can't discuss it on the
telephone ... very well, let me make it easier for you
... Is Farouk Hamzaoui involved? ... You can't say ...
I presume that means he is ... you still can't say ... all
right, let me change the subject ... What is Abdul
Farhaz doing in London? ... He's dead? ... How very
astonishing. I saw him the other day ... in Soho ... a
couscous takeaway shop, stuffing himself as usual
... I was chatting casually with Commander Sidney
Mudgeon, the new head of the Anti-Terrorist
Squad, and he's practically convinced that the bomb-
ing over here yesterday bears the mark of Abdul

Farhaz. You still think he's dead? ... Just as well I
called you in that case ... The bombing in London
was claimed by the Martyrs of the Seventeenth of
September ... could that be Farhaz's new splinter
group? You're still sure he's dead. Who told you?
Farouk Hamzaoui? ... You don't remember ...
oh, it's common knowledge ... I suppose you
know that the bombing was the work of the
Martyrs of the Seventeenth of September? ...
No, no, that was later, many hours later. The police
here are sure it has nothing to do with Farouk
Hamzaoui ... not his style, according to Mudgeon ...
Mudgeon is wrong?' Hilary smiled, and allowed a
moment to elapse. Then he went on quietly. 'In
other words, the Brotherhood of the Crescent
Moon is Farouk Hamzaoui? ... I must draw my own
conclusions ... thank you, my friend ... No, I can't
come to Beirut at the moment ... I have no wish to
be a hostage ...

'Not only that, I have no confidence in the Church
of England's intercessions ... good-bye ... Oh, one
final word, dear friend ... take it from me, Abdul
Farhaz is alive and well, and in London ... give me a
little more time, I will procure for you his address
and telephone number ... My telephone number?'
Hilary reflected for a moment. It was too dangerous
in case there should be contacts between Beirut and
Scotland Yard. He was, thank God, ex-directory, out
of force of habit. 'Are you there? Have you something to write with? 946-2178. Right. Adieu.' They
were numbers he had invented on the spot.

He put down the receiver slowly, and began to think. He looked out over the narrow Soho street in which he had bought his flat. Even though it was a sunlit morning, one could just notice the rhythmic changes of intensity in the light as the neon-signs of the Oh La! La! strip parlour, red as blushes, and the Adamant Eve Health Spa reflected on the grimy walls. He suddenly noticed that the Greek tailor's shop dead opposite his window, A. Agnostopoulos, was suddenly empty, the windows open, the glacial strip lighting off. The old man hadn't been looking at all well lately, hunched over his ironing board. Some workmen began erecting a notice. Desirable Office to Let, Sole Agents, Harry Goldhill and Nephew. There was a telephone number, of course. In a flash, a grand design of ludicrous proportions spread itself like a tablecloth in the forefront of Hilary's imagination. It wasn't yet megalomania, but as a halfway house to the ultimate target it was more than merely serviceable.

Was such a thing possible, or did it exist only in fiction, in which time and tide, to say nothing of coincidence were fine-tuned by the author to suit the exigencies of plot? Initiative was over half the battle; Hilary knew this by experience. The ambition of the counter-puncher was merely to seize that elusive initiative once again, when the enemy had revealed his intentions. It was worth trying. Human beings had an engaging tendency to be slow-witted as individuals. When solitude was multiplied into a collectivity, the slow-wittedness increased. It stands to reason that on a national level, slow-wittedness is tantamount to an illness. The single miscreant always holds an immense advantage over the mass of his pursuers, that is unless he has the appalling bad luck to be caught in error, which has been known to happen on occasion, but only rarely.

Hilary lifted the receiver. He had the initiative. He dialled the number of Harry Goldhill's office, and asked for Mr Goldhill. 'I am ringing to enquire about the vacant office at No 88 ... yes ... exactly. Incidentally, what happened to Mr Agnostopoulos? I see ... did he have any relatives? No, I hardly knew him – I once had a pair of trousers altered ... Yes, I know the office ... a front-room, a back-room, and the key to a shared toilet ... and how much? ... That seems a little excessive, doesn't it, in view of the age of the building ... I mean, did Mr Agnostopoulos pay that? ... Really? ... Well, I'll take your word for it, Mr Goldhill ... Who is the landlord? ... The Oh La! La! Corporation ... I see ... part of Oh La! La! International, with Headquarters in Palma de Mallorca ... no, not a bit ... I will not be taking the office on my own behalf in any case. What? ... Oh my name is Gwynne ... (He made a quick pencil note of his name on a pad) ... Lionel ... yes ... I'm acting on behalf of Cedarex ... Import-Export ... Headquarters in Tunis ... Yes, right, it was in Lebanon, but Mr Boutros Abassouad emigrated to Tunis ... how did you know? ... Oh, Cedars of Lebanon – Cedarex ... right, right ... you'd make a good detective, Mr Goldhill ... a modicum of culture? You're too modest, sir. Can I come round to see you? Today? Four o'clock? Perfect, I'll be there.'

Hilary examined his finances. He had been frugal all his life, perhaps because he had never been left anything by any one, and the pittance paid him as pocket money at school was the last and only affluence he had ever known, enough for an occasional Fry's chocolate cream bar. But he had successfully invested even the money from his slender pension, and he was now well enough provided for to be able to astonish acquaintances after his death. He resolved to take out as short a lease on the tailor's shop as possible. If it couldn't be done quickly, it wasn't worth doing at all.

The haggling with Mr Goldhill was entirely to do with the longevity of the lease, not with the money to be paid. The meeting ended indeterminately, Mr Goldhill declaring that he would have to get back to Oh La! La! International, while Hilary countered that he had to consult Cedarex.

Before the next meeting, two days later, Hilary called the number he had for Ahmed Kress in Beirut. The voice was too close for comfort, and yet strangely distorted. It was not that of Ahmed Kress. 'Oh, it's you Glasp? You gave us a wrong number.'

'Did you expect me to give you the correct number?'

'There is always the telephone book.'

'I am ex-directory.'

'I see. Anyway, I am glad you called, if for no other

14

reason that I am able to inform you, my dear friend,
that Abdul Farhaz is dead and buried.'
  'How do you know?'
  'I shot him, and I buried him.'
  'Farouk Hamzaoui?'
  'You are mistaken.'
  'I recognize your voice. You share a number with
Ahmed Kress. Interesting . . .'
  There was silence.
  'How are all my cherished Brothers of the Cres-
cent Moon?'
  The other party hung up. There was no harm in
creating a little havoc in Beirut, although havoc was
at no time in short supply over there.
  Within twenty minutes Hilary called back.
  'You know too much about our affairs. Be careful,'
said the same voice as before, now breathless.
  'Be careful? Why?' Hilary laughed quietly. 'I know
relatively little, but I guess a great deal, invariably
with alarming accuracy. The fault must lie with you.
And then, if I may say so, if I know too much, you
know too little. Abdul Farhaz is alive and well and
somewhere in London. We spoke at length about
you, and the Crescent Moon. He says you are not a
bad man, just foolish, and careless —'
  'I shot Abdul Farhaz at point blank range!'
  'You must have been blinded by passion. Abdul
Farhaz is not even wounded. He has grown a beard.'
  'He was always clean shaven!'
  'I asked him how long he had had the beard. He

15

told me he grew it six months ago, while sheltering with the Druses.'

'I shot him two weeks ago, clean shaven, and he never sheltered with the Druses!' Farouk Hamzaoui screamed. 'As God is my witness!'

Hilary took on a pious tone. 'God is all our witness, Abdul. I can only say, to prove my friendship to you, and my loyalty to the cause of the Crescent Moon, that within two weeks I should have an address for Abdul Farhaz. When that happens, I will pass it to you. And you can do as you see fit. All I can tell you for the moment is that he despises you, says you are a dangerous liability to any organization you are involved with, since you are both indiscreet and stupid.'

There was nothing but a prolonged howl of rage on the line.

'I am only reporting what he said,' Hilary went on, steadily. 'I see it as my duty. And now , if you will excuse me – there is someone at the door. It may be him . . .'

Hilary hung up.

He was flushed with pleasure. He sat down and began a letter to Sidney Mudgeon, the new chief of the Anti-Terrorist Squad.

'Dear Mudgeon,' he wrote, 'it may interest you to know that the explosion outside the Bit O'Blarney knitwear shop was indeed the work of the Martyrs of the Seventeenth of September, from which I am a recent dissident, since I have lost my taste for violence ever since my brother, Ali Shamadji, was killed while priming bombs for that organization. I know the outrage was claimed by the Brotherhood of the Crescent Moon, but that is just bluff by the greatest bluffer of the Islamic world, Farouk Hamzaoui, who is not trusted even by the other Brothers of the Crescent Moon. Believe me, the criminal you are searching for is none other than Abdul Farhaz, my cousin once removed. He is in England at this moment, using the name of Mustafa Tawil, or, at times, Colonel El Mouawad. Hoping you arrest him soon,

I remain, etc.

Ibrahim Shamadji.'

Commander Mudgeon received the letter after a day and a half. The postmark indicated that the letter had been posted in Loughborough. Hilary had gone to the station, and taken the first available train to wherever it went. This turned out to be Loughborough. He had a mediocre lunch at a pub advertising a 'nouveau cuisine Anglais', which meant there was less of it and it cost more. Then he returned in time to sign the lease for the office for and on behalf of Boutros Abassouad, Cedarex, 121 Boulevard du Combattant Suprème, Tunis. He countersigned as Lionel Gwynne, The Olde Forge, 34 Balaclava Crescent, Yeovil.

He next invested in a few pieces of inexpensive office furniture, and added writing paper, a rather shabby second-hand typewriter, equipment for stapling. Outside the office, he placed a brand new board, announcing the door as the entrance to

Cedarex, Import-Export Company Limited (Great Britain), Sole Agent Mustafa Tawil. And as a final bonne-bouche, he affixed to the doorhandle a printed notice saying 'Out To Lunch – Back Soon'.

The lease was for three months as a mutually agreed trial period, to allow Mr Abassouad, who was ill at the time, the opportunity to come over to London and approve the premises. Hilary paid cash, to which Mr Goldhill had absolutely no objection.

Once Mudgeon received the mysterious letter he called in Detective Inspector Hovaday, in charge of the case.

Mudgeon, a short man with a tough, amusing face, announced the receipt of the letter to Hovaday, a taller, gangling, balding figure, over a cup of tea.

'Do we know where it was posted?'

'Well, obviously. Have you ever received a letter without a postmark?'

'It might have been delivered by hand,' Hovaday suggested.

'In that case, why did you ask me where it was posted?' Mudgeon hated sloppy thinking as much as Hovaday hated nitpicking.

'Loughborough,' Mudgeon announced, letting Hovaday off the hook.

'Loughborough?' Hovaday murmured, incredulous.

'Yes, Loughborough. Do we know any Arabs in Loughborough?'

'We hardly know any Arabs in London, let alone

Loughborough. There's probably the usual ration of Sikhs and Pakistanis.'

'In other words, you have no ideas?'

'Not yet, I haven't.'

'Aren't you going to ask me who signed the letter?'

'I was assuming it was anonymous.'

'Oh, why were you assuming that?'

'I was assuming that, had it been signed, you would have told me the name.'

Mudgeon paused to let his irritation subside. Then he glanced at the letter. 'Ibrahim Shamadji,' he said.

Hovaday dug a piece of paper out of the depths of his pocket, and smoothed it out.

'Would you mind repeating that?'

Should one have to? 'Ibrahim Shamadji,' he elocuted.

'No. No. That's a new one to me,' Hovaday said.

'How about the Martyrs of the Seventeenth of September? Have we found out what happened on the Seventeenth of September?'

'There I've made in-depth enquiries, from London University and our Arab sources.'

'Well?'

'Nothing whatever happened on the Seventeenth of September.'

'Nothing? No Israeli clampdown, no shoot-out, no minor-prophet's birthday?'

'Nothing. Which leads me to the conclusion that all these names are purely arbitrary, invented on the spur of the moment to give the impression the organizations are larger and more numerous than we could ever cope with. In fact, I wouldn't be surprised if most of them were composed of the same personnel. If what I suspect is true, I think the media is doing us a grave disservice in seeming to lend credence to all these different names.'

'Hmm. Do you include the Brotherhood of the Crescent Moon?'

'Hamzaoui's mob? Hamzaoui has been identified variously as a member of the Fraternity of the Black Tent, the Warriors of the Sacred Oath, the Shadow of the Minaret, and the Voice of the Prophet.'

'I see what you mean. Is he still number one suspect?'

'No. He's always a suspect, but according to our informant, he's still in the Lebanon, and a very frightened man.'

'Wasn't there a rumour that he's dead?'

'If we were to believe all the rumours, everyone's dead. A man called Abdul Farhaz is supposed to have killed Hamzaoui stone dead, but a little later Farhaz was himself killed by Hamzaoui, so your guess is as good as mine.

'They don't make it easy, do they?'

'No.'

Such was Hilary's experience of the English administrative mind, with its affectation of ignorance and cultivation of distance in the face of emotional or violent behaviour, that he could almost guess at the nature of discussions at Scotland Yard, although he would have drawn the line at some of the more fatuous aspects of the actual conversation, believing them to be close to caricature. However, he understood clearly the nature of Mudgeon's perplexity. As a consequence, he took another afternoon off, and wrote Mudgeon a second letter.

'My dear Inspector,' he wrote, 'as you may have noticed, I have decided that Loughborough was too dangerous for me, and so I have moved temporarily. It has come to my notice that Hamzaoui has discovered my whereabouts, and that, owing to the treachery of two of my surviving brothers, he knows of my first letter to you, and bears me a grudge to say the least. I am no longer safe, since he has told a reliable source that he will come to England personally to eliminate me, together with one of higher standing in terrorist quarters than myself. I refer, of course, to Abdul Farhaz, whose alias in England is Mustafa Tamil, although he may have changed it again at the time of writing. I will keep you informed with what I hear. Now, there is no road back. In the words of the ancient proverb, I have saddled the camel, now there is no alternative to crossing the desert. Your brother Ibrahim.'

Mudgeon glanced at the postmark. It had been posted in Devizes. Mudgeon sighed, ordered tea, and called for Hovaday.

At this point, fate took a hand. News summaries were interrupted to announce that an Iranian diplomat in exile, Dr Bani Pal, one time second secretary in Baghdad, had been shot by two men on a Vespa while coming out of a gentlemen's convenience near

Leicester Square. Witnesses spoke of two swarthy men escaping on the motor-scooter against the flow of traffic. The scooter was found abandoned in a car-park near Greek Street.

Hilary lost no time. He crossed the road to the office he had rented, and used its phone to call the night editor of another tabloid.

'Hello,' he said, 'it is about the murder of Dr Bani Pal tonight.' Hilary spoke with an Arab accent.

'Yes,' replied the night editor with tight lips. 'D'you know anything about it?'

'It so happens Bani Pal was a traitor to the cause.'

'What cause would that be?' asked the night editor, fishing in deep waters.

'The true cause,' shouted Hilary.

'I understand that, but I am not a Moslem, and I only have a very sketchy knowledge of the causes at your disposal. I presume you are Iranian.'

'Wrong.'

'Arabic then. You are a fundamentalist, right?'

'A Fundamentalist Socialist.'

'I thought they were incompatible.'

'Until final victory they are compatible. After final victory, we shall see.'

'But what organization do you represent?'

'I am the spokesman for the Heroes of the Promise.'

'Let me just jot that down.'

'No! If you jot it down, our conversation is over!'

'Don't do that. Tell me, why did you pick on our newspaper to deliver this information?'

There was no sin in having a little fun in the cause of duty. Hilary had always operated that way, even in his heyday.

'We selected your paper because we thought your questions would be more than usually stupid. We are disappointed.'

'I see. Well, that's quite flattering, isn't it? Incidentally, you said we. How many of you are there?'

'Would you not like to know.'

'You won't tell me?'

'A hundred million.'

'No, no. I mean members of your group.'

'There is more than one and fewer than a hundred million . . .' Hilary continued this banter voluntarily, since he expected that the night editor had jotted down a quick message asking someone in his office to phone the police, and for them to try and identify the number from which the call was coming. It was a risk, but he deemed that the time had come for the police to be given more information, if his plan was to succeed. Still, he didn't want to reveal everything at once.

'I will leave you now,' he said.

'No, no, don't hang up yet,' the night editor implored. 'I want to make a real story of this. Page One stuff. Stuff that draws attention to you and your work.'

'Oh yes, and meanwhile you have written a note to your assistant asking the police to make every effort to identify my telephone number. No thank you, I am no fool. I prefer to give you the number myself, 177-4230. Are you satisfied?'

'I am not interested in your number,' said the night editor, his voice betraying the fact he was writing furiously.

'I will even tell you my name if you will tell me yours.'

'I'm Stanley Bales.'

'I am Colonel El Mouawad.'

And he terminated the call.

It was two hours later that an anonymous caller to Scotland Yard claimed the same crime on behalf of the Brotherhood of the Crescent Moon. He was told that he was too late, as there was already a claimant, the Heroes of the Promise. The anonymous caller seemed highly displeased, and hinted that there might be repercussions. It was not clear to the Scotland Yard switchboard what this meant, but the brief conversation was at once relayed to Mudgeon, who was, as usual, having tea with Hovaday.

'177-4230,' he said. 'Things are beginning to make a vague kind of sense at last.'

'Have we identified the number?'

'It's a call-box in Soho.'

'Ah. Far cry from Loughborough and Devizes.'

'Yes. And the name of the caller was allegedly Colonel Mouawad.'

'Doesn't ring a bell, I'm afraid. Their names all sound alike to me.'

'According to the original Loughborough letter, Colonel Mouawad is a pseudonym for Mustafa

Tawil, who, in turn, is none other than a pseudonym for —?'

'Abdul Farhaz?'

'Got it. So that the Heroes of the Promise are none other than the Martyrs of the Seventeenth of September?'

'Correct.'

'You know, it's quite possible that the whole terrorist act is a one or two man operation. It's like a tympani player and a third flute calling themselves alternately the London Philharmonic and Foden's Motorworks Band.'

'I like that.'

'What do we do now?'

'I've sent around to all estate agents with properties to let on short leases in the general area of Old Compton Street.' He shuffled the cards on his desk, 'Jakes and Jakes, Blankatwalla Brothers, Damian Ruskin, Pole and Vatni, Harry Goldhill and the rest. Very soon we'll have a comprehensive list of recent short lease rentals. This should help.'

Just then, the phone rang. The switchboard reported it seemed to be coming from Beirut. Urgently Mudgeon took the call.

'Hello,' said a voice cautiously, 'is that Chief Commanding Detective Midgin?'

'Mudgeon.'

'Of the Anti-Terrorist Squad?'

'Who is that?'

'You don't know my name.'

'Care to take a bet?'

'At all events, I wish to protest with the greatest vehemence.'

'Oh? You too?'

'Is there someone else protesting with vehemence?'

'There would be if we gave them half a chance. There's been someone this morning protesting that the murder of Dr Bani Pal is the work of the Heroes of the Promise?'

'So it is.'

'Ah, you agree? You are therefore Hamzaoui?'

There was a pause.

'Let us be reasonable,' the voice appealed. 'I am not Hamzaoui. My name is Kress. Ahmed Kress. I deal in public relations.'

'Public relations?' Mudgeon said, incredulous.

'For undesirables as you call them, misguidedly,' Kress went on. 'For freedom fighters, for kidnappers, for revolutionaries in general. I try to improve their image.'

'Good God. How do you do that?'

'By proving, every now and then, that hostages are still alive. We send out video-tapes, unfortunately of very poor quality, in which they declare they are being well treated. I am the first to admit that these are counter-productive because of the poor technique. They give the impression of downtrodden people, speaking under duress, which is not the case.'

'Allow me to be sceptical on that score.'

'With my hand on my heart.'

'And the other round someone's neck?'

'You wrong me.'

'I thought you were angry.'

'It is not I who am angry, merely indignant.'

'Hamzaoui is angry.'

'You are informed?'

'I'm using my nut. Hamzaoui's angry because Farhaz is stealing his thunder.'

'Farhaz is dead.'

'That is not my information.'

'No?' Kress seemed genuinely thunderstruck.

'Why are you surprised?'

'I was at the funeral.'

'Was there a mistake?'

'The wife had to be supported.'

'Had she identified the corpse?'

'It was impossible to identify it. Hamzaoui saw to that.'

'Perhaps he had his reasons for wanting Farhaz dead?'

'Reasons?'

'Self-deception?'

'And you think — ?'

'I think Farhaz committed the recent crimes in London. It's him we are looking for. It's him we're going to get.'

'By all that is holy! All this is deeply offensive to the Brothers of the Crescent Moon who proclaim their culpability with pride. Can you not understand Hamzaoui's feelings? This is like a slap in the face.'

'There's no face I'd rather slap. If I succeed in that *and* the arrest of Farhaz, my cup will overflow.'

Mudgeon hung up, feeling, like Hilary before him, that he had created his ration of chaos in the heart of the crazy organizations in Beirut.

Shortly afterwards he received confirmation from Goldhill's that Agnostopoulos' old workshop had been leased very recently to a company called Cedarex, registered in Tunis, whose business was Import-Export. The signatory of the lease had been a Mr Lionel Gwynne, of The Olde Forge, 34 Balaclava Crescent, Yeovil.

It took a call to the Yeovil police to discover that there was no Balaclava Crescent in Yeovil, and a further call to Police Headquarters in Tunis to learn some news quite as edifying, namely that no company called Cedarex was licensed to trade in Tunisia.

'Careless, careless,' muttered Mudgeon. 'They've got very long memories, and no foresight whatsoever.'

Hovaday called in from his police car in Soho.

'Well?'

'Good news, if you can call it good. The sole agent of Cedarex is Mustafa Tawil. His name's on the door, in English and Arabic.'

'Any sign of life in there?'

'None whatsoever. The door's locked. There's a notice saying he's out to lunch. It looks like a very long lunch. What d'you want me to do – force an entry?'

'Not yet. Keep the place under surveillance. Incidentally Cedarex is not a legitimate company, and Mr Gwynne who signed the lease is a figment of someone's imagination.'

'Probably Tawil's.'

'Possibly Tawil's.'

From his window, Hilary had noticed a police car parked further down the street, and a certain coming and going to the entrance of Number 88. It was extraordinary, this gift of the police to proclaim their presence whenever they made the effort to be unobtrusive. There was something about their walk, their tendency to look both ways, and even upward, before entering a building, things which ordinary people would never do; their way of waiting for others to catch up with them; their way of looking into shop windows in order to follow the movements of those behind them, reflected in the glass, all this bellowed their presence.

The time was ripe. The police had bitten. Hilary called Beirut. It was Ahmed Kress who answered in a state of high agitation.

'Why did you not call, yesterday, the day before? Now? Who knows? It may be too late!'

'What is the matter?'

'Hamzaoui is like a wild animal, with my hand on my heart, may I turn to dust if I exaggerate!'

'What has happened?'

'In the absence of an accurate telephone number for you, he was reduced to telephoning that avowed colonialist Midgin, who talks with a paternalistic condescension which is unbearably humiliating to anyone with Farouk Hamzaoui's pride. This man insisted that Farhaz is still alive, and that Scotland Yard believes him to be a greater menace than he, Hamzaoui. You can imagine how intolerable such a claim is to one like Hamzaoui, who is used to being considered the greatest menace of all, and especially when it comes from Scotland Yard, an organization we were all brought up to admire thanks to Agatha Christie and Dorothy Sayers, and Madame Tussaud.'

'What can I do to help?'

'Farouk Hamzaoui swears to go to London himself in order to find out the truth.'

'Where is he now?'

'Downtown, fetching a Syrian passport.'

'I can make his task easier. I have found out the address from which Farhaz is operating.'

'It is well.'

Hilary gave him the address, and the nom-de-guerre, Mustafa Tawil, but emphasized that the information was for Hamzaoui's use only, and must be kept secret, most especially from the police.

'In his present mood, I cannot guarantee. He is capable of killing me, even of killing himself, out of sheer exasperation. He is not a sane person. But perhaps your information will calm him. I live in hope. Believe me.'

'But he is determined to come to London?'

'Once he has decided on which passport to use, it usually means his mind is made up. I only hope he calls here before going to the airport, otherwise ...'

'He must pack a bag —'

'Since when? He likes to say he is always prepared to leave at a moment's notice, to the next destination or the next world. That is the lot of the combatant.'

Hilary had to work with the greatest dispatch. He recognized that the psychological moment had arrived, and while subtlety and clarity were still essential, sheer speed was also necessary. He quickly wrote a third and final letter to Mudgeon.

'My Brother,

Devizes having equally become too hot for comfort, I have moved once again, to where I can disappear more easily in the crowd. Hamzaoui, a man of undoubted courage but of dangerous volatility, is determined to settle accounts with Farhaz, who, he feels, has cheated him out of two major outrages. My informant in the Bekaa Valley tells me the hit squad is even now on its way to London, led by Hamzaoui personally, and that he will most probably use a Syrian passport to enter this country. I beg of you as a brother, do not attack Farhaz headquarters too soon. By being patient, you may capture even bigger game than the cursed Abdul, to wit, Farouk Hamzaoui and a handful of his most notorious henchmen, under whatever name they may today exercise their perfidy. As the saying goes, speed is the falcon's reward, patience the falconer's . May your steps be guided.

Your wellwisher
Ibrahim Shamadji.'

'He may be right at that. I like the falconer bit,' Mudgeon mused.

'Still Devizes?'

'No. Get this. Edgware.'

'Edgware? He's getting bolder.'

'He's covering up his traces. Now he's in a hurry. Things are moving fast. He hasn't the physical time to go as far afield as Loughborough or Devizes.'

'D'you think so?'

'I do think so. I even sometimes worry if he's really an Arab. Those proverbs sound a little too Arabian Nights to be true.'

'Who could it be?'

'I don't really care that much. If he goes on doing our work for us in this way, he deserves a medal.'

'Have we contacted H.M. Customs?'

'Yes. We asked for notification of all Syrian passports, but asked for the holders to be let through.'

'We'll follow?'

'Right.'

Towards the late afternoon, word came from Heathrow. A single Syrian passport, together with an Egyptian one, a Cypriot one, an Algerian one, and one from Oman, all the owners pretending to have nothing to do with one another until after Customs, when they left in the same car rented from Hertz. The car was an Austin Montego KRC 217D. It was followed discreetly into the West End, until it was left in Soho Square. The five inmates, four men and a girl, all of whom could have answered to that usual

description of swarthy, made their way to a Leba-
nese restaurant in one of Soho's minute backwaters,
the Byblos. Here they satisfied their nostalgia for
that only recently left behind, evidently waiting for
evening to turn into night.

Hilary felt a sensation in his bones which took him
back to the rare peaks of excitement in his active life,
and as he sat at his window in the darkened room, he
savoured the tension in the pit of his stomach, as
well as the temptations of folie de grandeur. Did
Nero have a better seat in the Colosseum than this
Royal Box looking deep into the heart of the stage he
had created himself? At the moment it was still dark,
but if all worked out as he felt it must, it would soon
be a hive of activity, a lethal clash of gladiators, for
his entertainment alone. All it needed was for the
curtain to rise.

He reflected, as he sat by his window, and the cool
evening air blew gently on to his face, making it feel
newly shaved. Revenge. That, he decided, was his
motive. There must have been moments when all
those dodderers in retirement cottages and shacks
had felt the same urge, but few of them had had the
guts, the fantasy, the sheer intelligence to have an
actual plan, and to put it into operation. Granted,
there had been a book, even books, not only from the
actual old boys in the field, as it were, but from those
self-styled experts on the fringe of the intelligence
world, those oracles consulted by less responsible
newspapers in moments of drama, who made a
handsome living out of their presumptions of

knowledge there where nobody knew the whole truth.

It is always presumed by avid readers of fiction, including fiction cleverly dressed up as fact, that the intelligence community is practically infallible. Of course, mistakes occur. That is a guarantee of humanity. But on the whole, the intelligence services enjoy the reputation of being what their name suggests, the cream of all that combines courage and intellect. Hilary knew better.

He still remembered with annoyance being called before Sir Aubrey Wilkett, then head of MI5, in order to be briefed on his new mission, back in the Fifties.

'You are to go to Persia, in order to use your undoubted talents to help destabilize the government of Dr Mossadeg. You doubtless know the situation out there as well as I do.'

'I know the Iranians are attempting to get rid of the British oil interests.'

'Who's doing that?' Sir Aubrey had barked, fearful that he might have missed something vital in the situation.

'The Iranians.'

'Who are they?'

'They used to be called the Persians.'

'Used to be? Used to be? Listen to me, young man, as far as I am concerned, they still are the Persians, and always will be. I am sick and tired of their constant attempts to confuse the issue. What an absurd idea, to change the identity of peoples after eons of history? Is my wife's cat a Thailandic cat? No sir, it is not. It is a Siamese cat, and will be for the span of its natural life. Is my mother's dog – yes, I still have Mother – she's ninety-six, God bless her – is her dog a Beijingese? Not as far as I'm concerned. It's a particularly disagreeable dog. I don't see why it should be encumbered by an unpronounceable breed as well.'

Hilary had protested that he was, perhaps, not the ideal choice for the job, since he spoke no word of . . . Persian. Sir Aubrey waved the objection away with a vague yet peremptory gesture.

'Oh come, you are an expert on that part of the world.'

Incredible how the British divide the world into indefinable parts when a global view of things is called for; parts which include absolutely incompatible elements, foreign to each other, which evidently require policing and other interference by those with experience in such matters.

Sir Aubrey considered Dr Mossadeg a potty old fool in pyjamas, who felt ill every time he ran out of arguments. Hilary, for ever bearing the unseen marks of his birth in a railway station, in 'that part of the world', tended to regard the same man as an heroic figure, attempting to rid his country of foreign influence. It was not only because he didn't speak the language, but certainly also because neither his heart not his talent were fully engaged in his reprehensible instructions that he was arrested before he had had time to do any damage, and after a couple of miserable weeks in an Iranian prison, sharing his cell with an American agent captured under similar circumstances, and who proclaimed his patriotism with pathetic insistence, as though he believed Hilary might be a plant to test his worth, he was allowed to return home.

'Hard cheese,' said Sir Aubrey, who regarded the misadventure as the luck of the game.

Later Hilary was sent to Egypt in order to help inflame the Egyptians against Colonel Nasser on the eve of the Anglo-Franco-Israeli complicity at Suez. He was even less qualified for this mission, ironically by virtue of the fact that he knew the language, and therefore understood fully the depths to which the provocateurs had sunk. He had an automatic understanding of the aspirations of the downtrodden and of minorities for self-expression. In a sense, he was a minority of one. His playground had been Arabian streets; his earliest fun had been had with grinning, shrieking urchins, whose ebullience he had shared until forced into the mould of quiet decency in what he was told was home.

He was forced into being a minor instrument of Eden's blind hatred of Colonel Nasser, and he hung back like a sulking child. It was perhaps the affair at Suez which more than anything crystallized Hilary's thinking, and gave his inherent resentments direction and focus. It happened several times that men of distinction had been forced to resign their seats in Parliament because they had been shown to have lied; yet Eden was given a peerage when his blatant lie to Parliament had disastrous consequences to his Government and to himself. A lie about a personal matter was evidently worthier of condemnation than a lie about a public event, in the course of which many innocent lives had been lost.

Since the beginning of conquest as a policy of state, colonial powers had been guilty of acts of terrorism, such as summary executions as an example to others, or the arbitrary destruction of villages. And yet today, terrorism only seemed to apply to forms of intellectual exasperation culminating in hostage-taking, booby-trapped cars, and hiding suitcases in public places. All such actions are finally bankrupt, and there is no difference between them except, at times, the scale of the operations. Just as the word democracy is now used by widely differing political opinions to describe widely differing social structures, so terrorism has been an instrument of repression since the earliest territorial burglaries. Hostages had been taken long before Richard Coeur de Lion languished in an Anatolian castle, waiting for the ransom to be paid. Innocents have been massacred from the dawn of recorded history, and still today men, women, and children are killed, not as a result of their culpability, but as an example to others. To be permanently shocked by such events is to be ignorant of history, or else it is just demagogic humbug. There are never as few as double standards at work. Standards are as variable as the weather, and deserve a scale of their own, taking into consideration local conditions, prevailing prejudice, climatic changes, and precedents.

These were values which Hilary was not expected to have. Nothing in his education had been instrumental in building such a personal view of things. It was due to his isolation from others, the accident of birth, often more dangerous to peace of mind than all other possible accidents.

A light switched on in the Cedarex office broke his reverie. Just as he saw the first hooded man breaking into view with quite unnecessary violence, seizing a fistful of meaningless papers on the desk, there was a furious but abrupt hammering on his own front door. He was as annoyed as someone woken from a deep sleep, and stumbled over the furniture in the dark, eager to put an end to the interruption.

'What is it?' he called out, angrily.

'Police,' came the reply.

An ice cold stalactite of reality touched a nerve.

'What do you want?' he asked.

'Open the door.'

He did so cautiously, after glancing backwards, and noticing that the lights had gone out again. They couldn't have slipped out of the trap?

In the doorway stood two men, grotesquely attired in the lunar outfits of modern conflict, grasping plastic automatics, and standing in attitudes of studied alertness.

'We've got to use your window. This is urgent.'

Hilary had not foreseen this. He would have to improvise with great consistency. The policemen advanced into his room. One of them stopped, suspicious.

'Sitting in here with the lights off, were you?'

'I often do.'

The other policeman took his place at the window. 'There's the window, Geoff, look.'

'Whatever you do, don't turn on the light,' said the other, to Hilary.

'I wouldn't dream of it,' replied Hilary, 'I was about to call the police in any case. There's something suspicious going on over there. Masked men.'

'Saw them, did you?' asked the man called Geoff.

'Must have been while we was on the stairs,' the other remarked.

'Yes, I saw them – at least, I saw one of them.'

There was a pause.

'You said as how you were about to call the police, and yet you wasn't too keen to let us in,' said Geoff.

'It's not my flat, you understand. The owner's away. Kindly lent it me. I can't take every decision.'

'Who are you?'

Hilary was eager to put an end to his position of subservience. Initiative. Initiative, the all-important.

'Colonel Crisp,' he said.

'Well, I'm sorry about this, sir,' Geoff muttered. 'If I were you, sir, I'd go to another room.'

'I think I know how to behave under gunfire,' Hilary said, hoarsely.

'I bet you do, sir. Then you'll know you'd be best off lying on the floor.'

'Not necessarily. It all depends what kind of gunfire we may expect.'

'These are desperate men.' It was the other man who spoke.

'Arabs, are they?'

'Yes, as far as we know.'

There was another pause for vigilance.

'Who does own this flat?'

'Friend of mine, delightful fellow, Hilary Glasp. He'll be sorry he missed this. Expert on the Near East. He's in America at the moment, lecturing on it. There's irony for you.' Torchlight appeared on the walls of the room opposite.

'Thank God, they're still there,' muttered Hilary.

'Why d'you say that, sir?' Geoff enquired.

'Pretty obvious, isn't it?' Hilary replied, not bothering to disguise his irritation. 'Once the police let them out, it'll evolve into a street fight, and there's always a risk innocent bystanders may get hurt. Confine them to that room, and it's like limiting the spread of a disease.'

'The street's been cordoned off.'

'People live in this street. As soon as anything happens, or even now, by virtue of being cordoned off, people will appear at windows and in doorways. You know how irrepressibly inquisitive —'

Hilary was interrupted by a single rifle shot.

Geoff lay as tense as a gun-dog. He slowly screwed a cup on to the end of his rifle.

Machine-gun fire came from the Cedarex window, aimed at the street. There were shouts, so short, so raucous, as to carry no message or indication of their origin. A voice suddenly bellowed a crackling message from a walkie-talkie Geoff had with him.

Geoff fired a tear-gas bomb across the street. It was a good shot. There were more shouts and curses, as well as a female scream. Then some coughing.

As the gunfire increased in intensity, the voice laced with static continued its litany on the walkie-talkie.

Suddenly Geoff said, 'Right.'

Both men opened fire from Hilary's window into the dark office over the street.

'That may have done the trick, with any luck,' Geoff muttered.

A hail of fire invaded Hilary's room, shattering ornaments, bringing pictures down, and lodging bullets in the wall.

'Are you all right, sir?' cried Geoff.

'Aren't you going to fire back?' shouted Hilary, brilliant in the role of the outraged Colonel Crisp.

Geoff and his colleague did what was commanded, until the voice on the walkie-talkie became strident.

'Hold your fire,' yelled Geoff.

There was an unexpected silence.

Then a single light went on over the way. The bulb had miraculously survived the fusillade. A policeman appeared in the pale glow, looking down on the floor, and moving with caution.

'It's all over,' Geoff announced. 'You can put the light on, sir.'

Hilary switched the lights on, and nothing happened. He felt the broken glass under his shoes.

'They got my light bulb,' grumbled Hilary. 'You didn't get theirs.'

'WE got them,' Geoff replied. 'They didn't get us.'

'That's true enough,' Hilary granted. Crisp mustn't be made to seem a fool, merely a pragmatic man of action.

'Who's going to pay for all this?'

'There'll have to be an assessment, and a report.'

'And the usual infernal delays, of course. I don't know how I'm going to break this to Glasp.'

'It'll all be dealt with according.'

'According to what?'

'You know, sir. According. It was just not Mr Glasp's day, was it?'

'Oh, I don't know.' Hilary allowed himself a trace of amusement. 'On second thoughts, I think Glasp will be furious to have missed the fun.'

'Fun?'

'Wasn't it?'

The marksmen left, refusing a half-hearted invitation to a cup of tea, and Hilary was left alone. He went to the kitchen, fetched a step-ladder and a new light bulb. He found the fixture itself damaged, and lit a candle which he kept for emergencies. In its flickering and mournful light he saw that the damage was considerable. An occasional lamp by the fireplace had been shattered; there were holes in the wall and ceiling, from which some plaster had fallen; two pictures had been torn off the wall.

It had been exciting all right, but hardly the kind of excitement he had bargained for. Gone was the Olympian detachment, the intention of working the strings so that the puppets would perform for him alone. He had had to share his Royal Box with unwelcome company, and he had inadvertently become a target for reprisals. And now he would have to think of the insurance, and all sorts of other imponderables. It was important that Colonel Crisp vanish, and Hilary Glasp return appalled to his mutilated home.

He felt tempted to go out, to take in a film perhaps, anything to change his ideas. It would give him pause, and the inspiration would begin to flow again, unaffected by the events which had crowded in on him with suffocating intensity. He did not really care for the movies, except as a diversion, a pastime. The morality of the ancient laws, in which virtue was rewarded, and villains brought to book, seemed to him so far from life that it might even corrupt that mysterious family for whom the cinema hoped to cater in showing them a cloud-cuckoo-land far from the sordid realities which surround us all. Upbeat optimism seemed to Hilary almost indecent. And recent events had done nothing to colour his vision, at least not in rose colours. It was time to take a break. He extinguished the candle, and prepared to go out. The street was still cordoned off, and there were police everywhere. Never mind, it was dark now. Hilary thought he would risk it. He went to the door, and looked through the spyhole. There was a man loitering in the half-light of the corridor. Hilary noticed him because he was smoking.

'Who's there?' Hilary called, his voice trembling with annoyance.

'Ernie Bask.' And the man added the name of the tabloid to which Hilary had phoned his first message on behalf of the Martyrs of the Seventeenth of September.

'What do you want?'

'A picture of the damage.'

'Well, you can't have it!'

'Don't you think the public deserves to be informed then?'

'The hell with the public. And the hell with you. You don't represent the public. On the contrary.'

'Who is that? Mr Glasp?'

'No!' Hilary shut his eyes in exasperation. He had hoped to kill off Colonel Crisp. Now he couldn't afford to.

'I'm a friend of Mr Glasp's, if you must know. I can't allow you in without his permission.'

'When's he coming back?'

'I'm not free to say.'

'Does he know what's happened?'

'I have managed to reach him, yes.'

'Where is he?'

'He's been in America.'

'Is he still there?'

'What business is it of yours?'

'I need a few more details for my story.'

'Look. Leave me alone. This is an invasion of privacy. Kindly go away.'

'You won't let me in?'

'No, and I'm not coming out.'

'What's your objection?'

'They are too many to enumerate. I'm a recluse.'

'Can I quote you on that?'

'How have you the nerve to ask? You'll invent whatever you like, whatever suits you. You always do.'

The man sniggered slightly.

'I admit there's a degree of fantasy goes with this job, but if people like you collaborated with us, that might not be necessary.'

'If you don't go, I will call the police.'

'It was the police who told me what happened. Told me your name was Colonel Cripps, or Crisp.'

'Then why did you ask me if I was Mr Glasp?'

'There's the name Glasp under your bell.'

'Good-night.'

'You're not going to change your mind?'

Hilary didn't bother to answer. He double bolted the door, and returned into his dark flat. The last thing he could afford now was a picture of himself in the papers. He could already visualize Mr Goldhill seeing the picture, and going to the police with the news that he was Lionel Gwynne, who had rented the office on behalf of Cedarex. He simply could not afford any mistake of that kind now. The only weapon left against the photographer in the hallway was sheer boredom. He had to abandon his idea of going to the movies until enough time had elapsed for other stories to supplant the battle in Soho in the headlines. He went to the kitchen, drew the blinds, and heated himself a tin of macaroni cheese. Nothing provokes hunger like adversity. He was a prisoner in his own flat, an unbearable degradation of his euphoria. Suddenly he was on the defensive, being careful not to linger too close to windows, which he imagined to be focused in the sights of secret photo lenses hidden in the night.

Highly nervous, he ate his miserable supper, dropped the plate and fork into the sink, and retired to his bedroom. Once again, he drew the curtains before putting on the lights. He switched on the little portable television set, fiddled with the aerial, and waited for the news.

It was, of course, dominated by the events of the evening. Details of the pavement, with chalk lines enclosing areas of splashed and trickled blood, made other aspects of the battle horribly vivid, aspects of which Hilary had not till then been directly aware. There were shots of a wounded Arab being taken away in an ambulance, and a brief interview with Mudgeon. The whole affair was portrayed as a triumph for the Anti-Terrorist Squad, and it was hailed by the Prime Minister as 'a new and vibrant phase in Britain's war on terrorism, and an example to other nations'.

Hilary hit a bedside table with his fist. He shouted out aloud. It seemed to him like a breach of copyright, this expropriation of his festival of irony, his gesture of derision. How dare the self-satisfied, smug establishment claim the authorship of a precise and painstaking plan, as carefully conceived as a railway timetable? (How proud his father would have been of him.) But then, the whole point of it was that it was secret, at times theoretical, at times pragmatic, but always profoundly personal and, naturally, intelligent. It even showed of what a man is capable when operating alone. How different the outcome to the disasters of Egypt and Iran (beg pardon, Persia), when under the orders of boneheads!

It was the 'example to other nations' which really touched Hilary on the raw. It was he and he alone who was the example, and yet he was destined to remain anonymous, no more than a filling-station attendant who did his job while the nobs sat chatting in the car, oblivious of his existence. He spent his time that evening divided between bitter indignation and relapses into feelings of resignation and impotence.

He woke still sitting in a chair, his glasses on, the lights as they were the night before. He must have fallen asleep when the conflicting thoughts had become too much to cope with. Sleep was better than the films, and cheaper. And now, here was another day. Who was he now, out of the copious dramatis personae he had invented for his drama? Before he had time to decide upon his identity, the doorbell rang. He glanced at his watch. It was after nine o'clock. He had only slept as long in a Tehran gaol. He went to the door, and took his glasses off to look through the spyhole. There seemed to be two men there, one hardly visible and distorted at the edge of the lens. The man in view did not resemble the journalist of the night before.

'Who's there?' he called.

'Colonel Crisp?'

What could he say? 'Who's there?' he reiterated, in a clipped, slightly breathy voice.

'Police, sir.'

Hilary's stomach seemed to shrivel.

'How do I know you're genuine?'

'Open the door on the chain, sir. I'll push the credentials through.'

Seemed reasonable enough. Hilary did what was suggested. An official document was pushed through the gap. Mudgeon?

Hilary opened the door, and retreated into the flat without looking Mudgeon in the eye. Mudgeon followed, and Hovaday shut the door behind him.

'Hm. Quite a bit of damage,' Mudgeon said. 'I doubt whether your insurance covers this sort of activity.'

'No. Soho has its violent moments, but they are usually single shots, not cannonades.'

Mudgeon introduced himself, and Hovaday.

'Obviously, there will have to be some sort of compensation. After all, it was the presence of police marksmen in the flat which occasioned this retaliatory fire.'

'Yes. Yes, it's very good of you to make that point, Mudgeon. It spares me from making it.'

'Oh, we're not in the business of scoring points or of evading responsibilities. According to my men, you behaved with exemplary courage and sangfroid.'

'That's very good of you,' Hilary muttered. And as an afterthought, 'Sangfroid, what a lovely word it is.'

'I've not had much occasion to use it, in my career.'

So he was to be flattered, and eventually reimbursed. There was a definite danger in remaining Colonel Crisp a moment longer.

'Where is Mr Glasp?' Mudgeon asked.

'Glasp? Why do you ask?'

'You seem to take a proprietorial interest in the damage done to this room. In that case, you must be very close to Glasp.'

Hilary decided on a bold move. After all, the police understand deception, and the frequent need for it.

'I am closer to Glasp than you think.'

'Really? I'm ready to wager you are Glasp.'

'What makes you say that?'

'There is no Colonel Crisp on the active list at this time. There's a Major Crisp, an invalid, living in Singapore. He's retired, Secretary of the Raffles Club.'

Hilary smiled. 'There's a certain advantage in choosing Smith.'

Mudgeon hardly smiled. 'Not really. Smith is immediately suspect. Crisp isn't.'

'Well, that's that.'

'Why did you feel impelled to assume a false identity – or is it a habit of yours – or a malady?'

'I didn't want the police in here, but if they had to come, I thought I'd give myself a little authority.'

'Very good,' Mudgeon admitted. 'It certainly worked. The lads were suitably impressed. One of them even remarked that they don't make 'em like that any more.'

'Sounds as if he'll go a long way.'

Mudgeon allowed a pause to elapse. Then he smiled, a little wryly.

'Who are you now, Glasp or Crisp?'

'Glasp,' Hilary retorted sharply. Mudgeon walked about the room, looking at things.

'You are a retired member of the British Intelligence Services.'

'I cannot speak about my past.'

'Oh?'

'Stands to reason. Once I am not permitted to write about it – as some have done – it follows that I am not allowed to talk either.'

'Yes, you're right. I hadn't thought of that.'

'I am instructed to think about it all the time.'

'What d'you mean?'

'The Government takes secrets very seriously, and the secret that there are no secrets left, most seriously of all.'

'Do I detect a trace of bitterness?'

'A trace?'

There was another pause.

'You speak Arabian.'

'The language is Arabic.'

'Yes, I know.' Mudgeon smiled engagingly.

'You wondered if I did?'

'You worked out there, didn't you? During the war and afterwards?'

Hilary's silence indicated that, in his estimation, that information fell under the Official Secrets Act. Mudgeon sat down, and made a gesture towards Hovaday, who produced a list.

Mudgeon studied it for a moment.

Hilary's face was drained of all expression.

'Does the name Farouk Hamzaoui mean anything to you?'

'...'

'Or Abdul Farhaz? I hope I do the pronunciation justice?'

'...'

'Have you any friends among the Martyrs of the Seventeenth of September?'

'...'

'Do you know anyone in Devizes?'

'...'

'What are you permitted to talk about?'

'Ask the Prime Minister. I don't want to put a foot wrong. It's too dangerous these days.'

Mudgeon smiled again.

'I admire a man who's good at his job – or rather, who was good at his job.'

Hilary smiled back.

'I wish I could return the compliment.'

'Oh?'

'You have done a lot of homework, I'll give you that. A bit too much if you ask me. But I don't think – if you will permit a criticism – I don't think it is good police work to play all your cards at once.'

Mudgeon spoke very softly.

'What makes you suppose that I have played *all* my cards?'

The doorbell rang.

'On cue,' Mudgeon said. 'It's uncanny.'

Hovaday nodded.

'Hovaday, I'd be grateful if you open the door. I feel Mr Glasp will not wish to open the door. He might be tempted to become Colonel Crisp again, and then there'll be no end of trouble.'

Hilary made a move towards the door, but Hovaday was quicker.

'How dare you —'

Hovaday let Mr Goldhill in.

'That's him!' Goldhill cried.

'That's who?' Mudgeon asked.

'That's Lionel Gwynne.'

'Lionel Gwynne?' cried Mudgeon in mock surprise. 'Not *the* Lionel Gwynne, of The Olde Forge, 34 Balaclava Crescent, Yeovil?'

'Is that the address he gave?' Goldhill asked. 'I can't remember offhand.'

'That is *his* address. The house belonging to Lionel Gwynne. He often has house-guests there. A Colonel Crisp, a Hilary Glasp, and a charming young foreign gentleman, Mr Ibrahim Shamadji,' Mudgeon said.

'Sounds like an Arab,' Goldhill declared.

'It is.'

'My God, look at the damage!' Goldhill exclaimed, suddenly noticing the bullet holes. 'Was that part of the – my God! Who's the landlord this side of the road?'

'I own my flat,' Hilary said.

'Then why did you give an address in Yeovil? Where is Yeovil anyway? Is there such a place?' asked Goldhill.

'I think two detectives on the case are sufficient, Mr Goldhill,' Mudgeon suggested. 'I don't want to embarrass Mr Glasp further by seeming to subject him to cross-examination. I just asked you to stop by at your convenience this morning in order to identify Mr – this gentleman.'

'Well, there's no doubt about it, this is Mr Gwynne, and I'd be willing to testify to that effect in a court of law.'

'There'll be no need of that,' Mudgeon said hastily. 'He's done nothing wrong.'

'Who's Glasp then?' Goldhill asked.

'It's too long to explain.'

'It said Glasp below the bell.'

'Yes, well, it would have done.'

'Is Glasp Gwynne?'

'And, no doubt, vice versa.'

Goldhill whistled. He evidently had an aptitude for deduction.

There was a long silence after Mudgeon finally

succeeded in sending Harry Goldhill back to his office.

Then Hilary spoke, very gently, and tentatively.

'You said I'd done nothing wrong ...'

'If what I suspect is true, you mounted an almost perfect police operation, always on the confines of illegality, exactly how such affairs should be conducted. You took greater risks than we would have been able to take. There's not that much place for imagination in routine.'

Hovaday suddenly spoke, setting aside his subservience in a marked and intentional way.

'My boss even said, halfway through the investigation, that whoever was busy engineering this confrontation deserved a medal.'

'And I meant it,' Mudgeon added.

Engineering was a word of which Hilary approved. It suggested all the meticulous craftsmanship needed for the creation of opportunity, all the exquisite timing, all the deep knowledge of human reaction to bait, the rationing of information, the subtlety of gestures in this *corrida*. He warmed to this man, to both these men.

'You deserve a candid answer to your questions.'

'I may deserve it, but I don't really need it,' Mudgeon replied, and he smoothed out a notebook which he had taken from his pocket. 'Tell me if I'm right. We owe you for the damage to the flat. That has already been established. Apart from that, there must have been several expensive phone calls to Beirut?'

'There were indeed,' Hilary admitted, 'but since it was not in my interest to keep records, and since they were often from different phones, I haven't the faintest idea how much I spent.'

'We're not very meticulous in such cases. The available reimbursements would come from secret funds set aside for just such contingencies, and we could easily assess your expenses based on current charges. You also made some local calls to a couple of newspapers. Right?'

Hilary grinned a little grimly. 'Right.'

'And rail trips to Devizes, Loughborough, and as far afield as Edgware.'

'You got the order wrong.'

'I made no attempt to get it right. Can you think of any other expenses I might have overlooked? Oh incidentally – you travelled first class to all these places?'

'I travelled at the cheaper rate.'

'Since there is no record, I think you will find you travelled first. At least, that is how we intend to repay you.'

'That's very good of you.'

'So I expect a list – not necessarily a precise one, you understand – of all your disbursements on our behalf.'

'I can't expect you to repay the excitement, the fun, the exhilaration.'

'Fun? Well, we won't hold you up any further, Mr Glasp. We'll call sometime tomorrow – if you could have your list ready by then.'

He went to the front door, followed by Hovaday. Suddenly he turned. His face was unsmiling.

'I know exactly what you did and how you did it, Mr Glasp. But you spoke just now of fun, of exhilaration. I understand everything, except the motive. What was your motive?'

'...'

'Is that a breach of confidence too? Are you a man of quite unusual patriotism?'

'I ... I don't imagine so,' Hilary answered soberly.

'Are you a man who finds retirement irksome, boring?'

'Not particularly.'

'Do you miss the thrills of life in the Secret Service?'

'Thrills?' Hilary snorted, derisively.

'Are you taking some sort of revenge?'

'I never thought of it in precisely those terms.'

'Well, are you? On anyone in particular?'

'No.' Then he added, as an afterthought, 'They're not worth it.'

'They? You're taking your revenge on the whole damn shooting-match?'

'I wasted a great deal of time.'

'And now you're making up for it?'

Hilary didn't wish to answer any further questions. A new vibrancy entered Mudgeon's voice.

'Right. The casualties were four dead among the terrorists, and one pretty badly wounded. On the police side, there was a single bullet wound. The man's life is not in danger.'

56

'I'm glad to hear it.'

'How did you know, how could you be sure, that the result wouldn't be exactly the opposite? Four police dead, one wounded. One terrorist grazed by a bullet?'

Despite the hardness of Mudgeon's voice, it was too easy to reply, for once. Mudgeon's defences were down.

'Please don't be too hard on me if I took the competence of the police for granted,' Hilary said.

Mudgeon's stern expression melted into a wide, generous smile.

'At least admit', he said, 'that you took an awful chance.'

'I merely emulated you. And then, luck played a part.'

It was exactly the right moment to be modest.

As an afterthought, Mudgeon said, 'You'd have no objection if I made my report available to the Prime Minister, I suppose? Initiative and individualism are at an extremely high premium at the moment, and I think your exploit may give a lot of pleasure in high places.'

'I can't imagine it to be of any interest. In fact, I had hoped that all this would get no further.'

'Discreetly. Discreetly, of course.'

'I should hope so.'

'You are ...?'

'What?'

'British?'

'What an extraordinary question.'

'No offence.'

Once outside, Hovaday complimented his chief.

'Bloody brilliant.'

'I thought he was going to offer us tea,' Mudgeon replied.

'That's the only thing you got wrong.'

The next day, as Hilary had anticipated, there were other attractions to draw the attention of the journalists. Four female torsos had been discovered in a disused quarry near Buxton, and the battle in Soho faded into history, and with it Hilary's initiative became a well-documented memory in his own mind. He went shopping as he had before, exchanged impressions of the great night with locals, and slowly fell prey to all the tiny nervous afflictions which herald old age. It was almost as though it had never happened.

In order to rekindle a few embers, he put a phone call through to Ahmed Kress in Beirut. He did this from his own phone. Now he had no tracks to cover.

Kress was sad rather than angry.

'With my hand on my heart, I did not weep a single tear when I heard that Hamzaoui was dead. He had become a burden to the cause, he was in many ways a madman, and I hated him as one can only hate one's brother. I am glad he is dead. And yet, I can never forgive you for the way in which he died, like a proud animal in a trap, and three brave people died with him, one of them a woman. And Kamal Azizi is a prisoner. Shall we ever see him again? All because of you. I thank you for ending the suffering of Hamzaoui, a thing beyond my power. And I wish never to speak to you again.'

Ahmed Kress ended the conversation. Hilary's face burned as though fevered. Never had humiliation taken such a palpable form. He thought not of the dead, but of their families and friends, for the first time, since Kress represented those who were not actually engaged in events, but those in the wings, wrapped in doubt, in ignorance, subject to rumours, and eventually, the mourners.

As a sop to his conscience, he sent £20 worth of white flowers to be placed on the presumed grave of Abdul Farhaz. He did this through Interflora, addressed to Farhaz's sister, whom he had known in better days.

The police paid up handsomely, the room was redecorated, yet Hilary felt uneasy about what he had done. What had started as an anarchic protest had ended as a gesture which was deficient in significance, lacking the necessary ingredient of logic, of moral posture. The shooting had blown out of all proportion something which was no more than a prank.

Hilary would have liked to forget the whole wretched incident. Then, surprisingly soon and quite unexpectedly, there came through the door a drab, buff-coloured envelope. It was On Her Majesty's Service. Automatically Hilary thought of taxes, and wondered what he had done wrong with all the fear which such documents engender in free societies. The printed letter within, far from asking for elucidations, wondered whether, if Hilary were offered an M.B.E., he would be willing to accept it. The highly placed person had looked out of the limousine after all, and smiled at the filling-station attendant. He glowed, no longer with shame, but with an extraordinary sense of elation. Here was a fact which would irritate his old colleagues in retirement, in their cottages in Hampshire, their hovels in the sun, their places in Australia. In a world of rancid secrets, they would wonder what he had done to have earned this honour, and the beauty of it was, they need never be told. They would squirm in their twilight, contorted with envy. His action had been given the necessary focus, even if it was entirely different from what had been his intention. It was, in fact, the very opposite.

Soon Hilary began to kid himself that the reason he had lured the terrorists into a trap was his insatiable ambition for some form of official recognition. Then, with an instinct inherited from his old profession, he began to fancy that he was being followed. As his ego swelled, so did his sense of persecution.

It was on the day that he took a taxi to Buckingham Palace, dressed in a rented morning-suit which smelled heavily of camphor, that he imagined for the first time that he could actually identify his shadow. The same vaguely defined features seemed to recur day after day, a man of medium height with a prominent jaw, dressed with the flagrant anonymity of a professional.

The ceremony at the Palace disappointed him somewhat. It was an anticlimax after the poignant exclusivity of the letter. There were so many other M.B.E.s, and there was nothing with a more dampening effect on Hilary's nascent sense of self-satisfaction than this huge group of people, chattering like tourists awaiting the departure of their coaches. He knew nobody, and felt acutely lonely in this sea of victors and their families.

The actual contact with royalty was as brief as an injection, and it was on his way out, and during his inability to find a cab in the vicinity of the Palace, that Hilary realized for the first time with what refined cruelty Britain rewarded her ill-wishers.

And his troubles were not over yet. It was while walking back towards Soho, the odour of mothballs still surrounding him like a halo, that he clearly defined the man walking behind him. From now on, he could identify him in a crowd. Hilary stopped in order to pretend to do up a shoelace. The man also stopped illogically in order to consult a newspaper which happened to be in his pocket. Hilary dragged out the moment. So did the man. When Hilary walked on, the man put his newspaper away, and walked on too.

Hilary reached home only to find the road up and police everywhere. A car bomb had exploded just in front of the building, shattering all the windows which had so recently been mended. The car itself was a wreck. There was debris all over the place.

Hilary hurried up the stairs to find his door open,

and his two friends from the Anti-Terrorist Squad inside.

'Well, you had a lucky escape,' said the senior of the two. 'Sergeant Unsworth, remember?'

'Geoff.'

'Right! It's O.K., you can go in. We've just been through your flat with some of our equipment. There's no trace of any more devices inside, but you can't be too careful. They often come in pairs.'

'Who did it?'

'Can't tell yet.'

'But why ... why?'

'I should call the Big White Chief if I were you. Oh, here's a greetings telegram we found on the doormat.'

Hilary opened it.

It read: Congratulations, You Certainly Deserve It, and was signed Mudgeon.

Before Hilary had time to telephone, his shadow, the man with the lantern jaw, appeared in the doorway.

'What happened then?' he asked the two others in a cosy North Country accent.

'Car bomb,' said Geoff, as he helped his mate to localize the broken glass.

'Go on. Here? Well, you was loocky, wasn't you? Couldn't find a taxi, could we?'

'You have been following me, haven't you?' Hilary asked.

'Not on Saturdays or Sundays. There's a pal of mine on t'week-ends.'

Hilary dialled Mudgeon's number as he talked.

'Why d'you say I was lucky?'

'They was banking on you being in, I wouldn't be surprised. They weren't to know taxis are scarce in St James's Park.'

'Who are they, in your estimation?'

'Terrorists, I'd imagine. Who else'd want to get you? Am I right, Geoff?'

'Right.'

Mudgeon was on the line.

'Thanks for your telegram.' First things first.

'I hear your flat is a mess again.'

'Any idea who did it?'

'I could ask you the same question. All I can tell you, Glasp, is that Kress swears it is not the Brotherhood of the Crescent Moon. With my hand on my heart, he says.'

'If he swears he has nothing to do with it, that is the best guarantee that he is deeply involved.'

'You know him better than I.'

'But ... what gave you the idea of contacting Kress?'

'You did, in a way.'

'You were more thorough than I thought.'

'Half our time is spent pretending to be inefficient in order to spend the other half efficiently.'

'You had me followed.'

'Yes. I thought this might happen sooner or later, although Kress swore you were beneath their dignity, small fish in a world of big fish.'

Mudgeon was evidently doing everything to make himself attractive.

'Does this not rather prove the contrary?' Hilary asked. He was still in his rented magnificence, and was in a mood to be considered big fish.

'If Kress is responsible, I agree. But is he?'

'Where did the car come from. Was it stolen?'

'Rented, at Heathrow. In the name of Ibrahim Shamadji.'

'What was that name?' Hilary's voice trembled despite himself.

'Ibrahim Shamadji,' Mudgeon enunciated.

'That's nonsense!' Hilary barked. 'It's a name I made up. Pure invention.'

'Is it? Seems not to be any more. Oh. Just a minute, old man, they've just pushed a bit of paper in front of me. Good grief. A man just telephoned Scotland Yard, claiming the bombing on behalf of the Martyrs of the Seventeenth of September.'

There was a silence. Hilary's face was ashen.

'What should I do?' he croaked at length.

'Honestly?'

'Honestly.'

'The world's a big place, for most people,' Mudgeon said. 'Portugal's popular, but it's rather close. There's South Africa. That's out of bounds for these boys, and the police are really hot. Or there's Australia.'

'You think I ought to clear out. To run?'

'Only for ten years or so. But why would you want to come back? Frankly, I won't be able to shadow you all the time. It's too expensive. Not worth it. And these boys from Beirut have an odd set of values. There's no shortage of targets for them, and yet they believe in revenge as a first priority. They're sentimental at heart, I believe. Is it the elephant who never forgets, or the camel?'

'The elephant.'

'Could as easily be the camel.'

'But why are they suddenly so vindictive? Kress thanked me for having got rid of Hamzaoui. He actually thanked me!'

'I know, but apparently it was the flowers for Farhaz which acted like a slap in the face. It seemed to them the final act of cynicism. An outrage.'

'And I meant it to be conscience money.'

'Well, there you are. I don't have to tell you about people, do I? They understand what they wish to, they interpret according to their own prejudices, and they kill for reasons of their own. Nothing makes any sense if you analyse it. The best course of action is to stick to your particular distortions of reality, and act accordingly. And above all, in our world, act quickly. Quickly rather than rightly or wrongly. Well, I must be off. And take my advice. Australia. Or New Zealand. Act quickly. Be good.'

Hilary changed from his formal suiting, and took a shower to get rid of its aroma. Then he drew the blinds before it was dark. New Zealand? He envisaged a mass of sheep, and began imagining in his daydream that one of them was earmarked to follow him.

It was a decision he had to make. Would he from now on be on the run, or would he be as fatalistic as the terrorists? He lifted the curtain. The police were just removing the remains of the rented car. Death would have come instantly to an occupant. It was a matter of a split second, and nothing to fear physically.

Moving to New Zealand would do nothing for his dignity. He would continue to wonder how far their vengeful arm could reach, and if ever they gave up the chase, he would feel abandoned to a grey anonymity, devoid of every human element which makes life worth living.

He too had to take his revenge, he decided. The M.B.E. was a momentary temptation to which he had succumbed. It was a beckoning hand before the cemetery of dreams.

With a sudden surge of energy, he sat down before a blank sheet of paper. Here would be something positive, something aggressive and true. He began a new chapter to his book, the one that would be discovered after his death, the most penetrating assessment of the life of an eavesdropper, M.B.E. As for his integrity, he would rediscover it somewhere between the as yet unwritten lines.

At one moment, he thought he heard someone at the door. After a hesitation, he ignored it, and went on writing.

A Nose By Any Other Name

For as long as she could remember, it had been the same. People had come up to her and, their faces suffused with tremulous but discreet emotion, had congratulated her on having such wonderful parents. Why then, she had wondered, and this with a growing intensity, why had she harboured a subdued resentment against them both? That was during adolescence. Now she knew.

The little family of three – she had no brothers or sisters – lived on the campus of a minor American university, in one of the smaller states close to the Atlantic seaboard. Professor Ramaz Atoulia, her father, was a great expert on international law, often consulted by obscure and exalted magazines appearing at odd times during the year, and read by people as obscure and exalted as they. His special expertise covered such rarefied areas as Kurdish village jurisprudence, and the legal systems of medieval Azerbaijan, Georgia, Armenia, Tadjikistan and other continuously shifting neighbouring realms, and as

such he was occasionally consulted by the State
Department prior to some decision or other.

On those great days, he would leave by train,
accompanied to the station by wife and daughter in
a taxi. Neither parent could drive, and so they had
never invested in a car. Both females were sworn to
secrecy, and the Professor would leave, wreathed in
his habitual smiles, to sprinkle wisdom liberally on
the arid soil of the capital.

The smiles, Thamar often reflected, were among
the most irritating features of both parents. Her
mother smiled practically all the time, for no under-
standable reason. Her father, however, had a vast
repertoire of smiles to fit a variety of occasions.
Among the most galling were those reserved for the
dispensation of wisdom, and for the dispensation of
common sense, the former meltingly serene, the
latter identical, but with a trace of controlled impa-
tience in the pale brown eyes. Thamar knew the
repertoire by heart, and knew which to expect as
occasions arose, which only made matters worse.

It was not that she didn't love her parents; it was
that she knew nothing else.

Not only did they not possess a car, but they did
not even possess a television, nor indeed a radio.
Without it ever becoming a theory, the Professor
instinctively agreed with Tolstoy that ideally a man
should be able to do everything for and by himself.
Instead of a radio, the Professor played the violin,
his wife, the piano, and from an early age Thamar
had been compelled, as though it were a necessity

for survival, to learn a 'cello a little larger than herself. Now, instead of listening to music, they made it.

The Professor was considered a man of great commitment to personal liberty, but since his wife obeyed his every whim even without being asked, it was difficult to tell just how easygoing the Professor really was. Certainly he was a man of nuance, adding shades of meaning even where such niceties were unnecessary, but that may well have been due to the defence mechanisms of international lawyers, which are often deployed without provocation.

It was on the 13th of July of a particular year that all of Thamar's secret resentments suddenly came into focus, and she knew, in a single flash, exactly what she needed to do to survive, and to discover herself. It was only a short while before her 21st birthday, and she had made plans to go out with some friends, who, she felt, were not real friends at all, but those who pitied her in some obscure way, and were therefore of a generous and understanding nature. She was probably wrong about this.

The Professor suddenly announced that Professor Buke, of the Faculty of Sumerian History, the Dornsteins from Political Science, and the Mandelzweigs (he occupied the Egbert Hornaman Swales chair in Economics) were coming to dinner that evening. At Professor Buke's request, there would be Mendelssohn, and the Dornsteins were eager for the Dvořak 'Dumky Trio'. Professor Mandelzweig had plumped for Beethoven's 'Archduke', while Mrs Mandelzweig had asked for something with a tune.

'But Papa,' Thamar said, 'I've accepted an invitation to go out with Josephine Turner.'

'Josephine who?' asked the Professor, making it sound as if he would have preferred another Josephine.

'Josephine Turner – you know – the daughter of the football coach.'

'Oh, Turner!' exclaimed the Professor, as though wishing that people would enunciate properly. 'Well, if you've accepted you've accepted.' The winning smile broke through the clouds, tinged with melancholy. 'It will merely mean that Mama has to cook unaided for seven people, as well as lay the table, and wash up, and there will be no music in my house tonight.'

'Why can't you and Mama play sonatas?'

'Sonatas? With half the burden instead of a third, having laid the table, cooked?'

'Why didn't you tell me ahead of time?'

'Why didn't you, my darling?'

'I shouldn't have to.'

'You still live at home. When you are married ... have a family of your own ...'

'I'll call the Turners.' Anything to avoid this embarrassing speculation about being married and having a family. On her way to the phone, she caught sight of herself in a mirror. 'I'm hideous,' she said aloud, and hoped that someone had heard. No one had.

It wasn't true that she was hideous. She merely had a nose which was a bit too long to be elegantly proportionate. Her lips were thick and sensuous, but the tip of the nose overhung the mouth, which gave her a tendency to scowl. It was a pity, because the upper part of her face could have been that of a great beauty. Her father had the same kind of nose, which sometimes made it seem as though he breathed through the filter of his pencil-thin moustache. Her mother's nose was almost identical, but with her expression of pervasive mildness, it gave her mouth a kind of sweetness, as though she were permanently tasting food of indefinable subtlety. Sometimes, as now on the phone, while muttering her excuses to the Turners, Thamar imagined a night of love shared by her parents, coiled round each other in nakedness, the spark which had engendered her existence, the existence of her and that of her 'cello. A sudden rage overtook her when she replaced the receiver. She would now be available for laying the table, cooking, washing up, Beethoven, Dvořak and Mendelssohn.

'The devils,' she hissed, 'they didn't give me a chance. They fell in love with each other's noses. They fell in love with themselves. A child of theirs didn't have a hope in hell! It had no alternative. It had to have that nose!'

And then, to save herself from any other thoughts she might regret, she took refuge in fantasy. 'Perhaps I'm mad,' she thought. 'Why would I be mad? Perhaps Papa and Mama are brother and sister.'

Certainly their relationship was much more like that than a relationship between man and wife. There was a kind of complicity between them, as though they had survived the same capricious upbringing and were now passing it on religiously, as a matter of tradition.

There was nothing surprising about the dinner itself. The cooking was based on pilaff, rice with raisins and nuts, and some charred bits of lamb which awakened ecstasies in Professor Buke, who was a widower: any kind of cooking reminded him of his late wife, which was both touching and a little morbid. After dinner, they settled down quickly to the music. They had not much to say to each other, since they saw each other very frequently in the course of daily events, and were not overly garrulous away from the subjects of their choice.

Professor Buke shut his eyes in expectation of the Mendelssohn. He leaned back, while the Dornsteins contented themselves with expressions of moderate solemnity, as though at prayer in a place of worship foreign to them. Professor Mandelzweig smiled with a kind of grim satisfaction, while his wife fidgeted with her handbag. She had clearly not wanted to come.

As the graceful Victorian filigree came to life, Thamar watched her parents, her mother disguising the fact that she was counting the bars with a suave negligence of manner, the flesh on her upper arms wobbling like a turkey's neck every time she hit the keys with some robustness, her father's eyes shut and eyebrows raised with the depth and penetration of his perceptions. It made Thamar wild with anger. For once, her pride in playing well was subjected to a spasm of revolt. She did something she had never done before. Deliberately, calculatedly, she played a wrong note.

Her father opened his eyes in surprise, then quickly shot his daughter a look of comprehension. To err is human. Her mother did the same, but not before seeking tacit confirmation from her husband. Professor Buke noticed nothing. The Mendelssohn came to an end to general applause. There was a little re-tuning before the Dvořak. Mrs Mandelzweig muttered something about an early start in the morning, and made an attempt to rise. The Professor suggested that they might play the Beethoven first, since Beethoven was the Mandelzweig request. 'It's even chronologically logical,' laughed the Professor.

'Hell no, you stick to your programme, Ramaz.' And he threw the keys of the car at his wife, who was not expecting the gesture, and dropped them. 'I'm sure the Dornsteins will drop me off home.'

'I don't want to disrupt everything,' said Mrs Mandelzweig. 'It's just that ...'

'The lady prefers big bands,' interrupted her husband.

'No. Not at all.' And after a moment of embarrassed uncertainty, Mrs Mandelzweig picked the keys up off the floor and hurried towards the door.

Since nobody seemed inclined to say anything, Thamar called out.

'Goodnight, Mrs Mandelzweig... So glad you could come.'

Mrs Mandelzweig stopped in amazement and answered Thamar. 'Goodnight, and thanks for having me.' And she left.

Professor Mandelzweig spoke in his voice of gravel. 'I'm sorry you found it necessary to say that, Thamar. If I seem to be rude, it's not because of anybody here present, but because of Beethoven. I like the guy. He had a hell of a lot to put up with from horses' asses, and I guess he deserves a little respect.'

'Without wishing any disrespect to the gentleman in question,' replied Professor Atoulia, after a moment, 'the Atoulia family will now attack Dvořak's "Dumky Trio".'

There was a smattering of applause, and the sound of Mrs Mandelzweig's car starting up on the drive.

The incident rambled in Thamar's mind, and towards the end of the third movement, in another curiously reckless moment, she deliberately played a wrong note, more blatant, more disruptive than before. This time she arranged to look perfectly normal and composed, and took in her parents' astonished glances without for a second meeting their eyes. She even insisted on her chosen path by playing the note wrong in the repeat as though her parents were wrong.

Naturally, nobody drew attention to the errors.

The Dornsteins agreed that Dvorak was 'one hell of a composer, in some respects, not better, but fresher than Brahms.'

'I'm not sure you can make comparisons in the stratosphere,' mused Professor Atoulia.

'There must be a possibility of critical appraisal, even in the stratosphere,' Professor Dornstein insisted.

'Are you fellows suggesting that Beethoven shares the stratosphere with the likes of Dvořak and Mendelssohn?' asked Professor Mandelzweig.

'To each his own stratosphere, *if* stratosphere there be,' pontificated Professor Buke.

Thamar listened to this argument, which was not lacking in the kind of absurdity of which only those of superior intelligence are capable, with her 'cello leaning on her leg. She knew there was still the 'Archduke' to come, and she was eager to be rid of it, to do the washing-up, and to go to bed. The others were smoking and drinking. It was the intermission.

'For what it's worth, I always have a vision of peasants when I play Dvořak, a vista of marble halls when I play Mendelssohn, and a feeling of Elysium at its most intimate when it's a question of Beethoven – does that sound ridiculous?' asked Mrs Atoulia.

'I'm rather glad you don't convey those images to the listener,' said her husband without evident cruelty, and added, on a more sincere note, 'You play far too well to tell us about the processes which lie behind it.'

That effectively shut his wife up.

'And what about the young lady with the 'cello?' asked Professor Mandelzweig, who was evidently an authority at getting rises out of females. 'What does she feel?'

'I feel absolutely nothing,' said Thamar, in tones of ice.

'I can't believe that that is true,' joked her father, but gave up the train of thought when confronted by the forbidding lack of expression in his daughter's face.

They played the Beethoven dutifully, but without great fire. The fun had gone out of it, and in view of the tenuous atmosphere, Thamar took great care not to make any more mistakes.

'Isn't that the greatest?' said Professor Mandelzweig as he rose to leave. 'Intimate Elysium, you just about said it all right there. Ala, I don't know what I'd do without your musical evenings. Food for the gods, that's what they are.'

'And we are the gods?' asked Professor Atoulia, with his usual brinkmanship, on the edge of humour.

'Who else?' cried Mandelzweig, struggling into his coat.

'Ala, Ramaz. It's been a wonderful experience,' added Professor Dornstein. 'And I mean that sincerely.'

'And I hope our young 'cello prodigy realizes what a wonderful family she has been born into,' added Mrs Dornstein.

Thamar's smile was small and frozen.

'She is shy,' said her father.

'If I was her, I'd be trumpeting my good fortune from the roof-tops,' replied Mrs Dornstein on a note of challenge.

'It is against our family tradition to trumpet anything from the roof-tops,' chuckled Professor Atoulia. 'We are Christian, not Moslem.'

This allusion was beyond Mrs Dornstein, who retired from the battlefield, to give way to Professor Buke, the widower, always the first to arrive and the last to leave.

'It would be insulting you to say it was a perfect evening as that somewhat boorish Aaron Mandelzweig suggests. The evening was better than perfect, by virtue of its human imperfections. The tempi in the Mendelssohn were slovenly at times, there was a lack of rigour in the Dvořak, there were several errors in the Beethoven – who cares? What matters is the human spirit which assailed these Olympian heights, and which failed as all human endeavours must fail, but by how little! Ah, how little! This is what the Sumerians understood with such extraordinary clarity!'

Thamar left the room, and began the washing-up.

'I hope the young person is not upset by my critique,' said Professor Buke softly.

'I don't think so. But on a point of accuracy, and now that she is no longer in the room, I can tell you that the errors occurred in the Mendelssohn and in the Dvořak. The Beethoven was note perfect,' remarked Professor Atoulia.

'I heard distinct errors in the Beethoven and not in either the Mendelssohn or in the Dvořak,' Professor Buke insisted darkly. 'Perhaps you are less attuned to Beethoven than to the others. Don't spoil an enriching evening by your obtuseness, please.'

Professor Atoulia was quite used to this. 'I would offer you one for the road, Tim,' he said quietly, 'but I believe you've already had several.'

Professor Buke began to sob quite suddenly. 'Am I drunk?' he enquired.

'Not drunk, but drinking.'

'God, if only Alma hadn't ... gone ...'

'I know, I know,' Atoulia consoled. 'Come on, I'll call a taxi. Leave the car here tonight. You'd best not drive yourself.'

'Can you ever forgive me?'

'What is there to forgive?'

'The Beethoven was superb. Piatigorsky, Feuermann and Janoš Starker couldn't have played it better. Right?'

'They couldn't have played it at all. They were all 'cellists.'

'Don't damn well interrupt me,' cried Professor Buke obstreperously, as Atoulia was trying to phone for a taxi.

'The Mendelssohn was ma ... majestic. Worthy of Cortot, Richter and all of that. The other fellow, the Yugoslav, you – oh, the hell with it – why don't you stick with something you can do?' Buke fell asleep.

It had been even worse before Alma went.

Lying awake in bed, Ala spoke to her husband in the dark. 'I've never known Thamar to make mistakes before.'

'No,' murmured her husband, reasonably. He had not yet had time to give his powers of deduction free rein.

'The second mistake shocked me more than the first.'

'Yes. Why?'

'She was shocked herself. The second mistake she seemed not to notice.'

'If it was deliberate?'

'Deliberate? A mistake?'

'It is perhaps her way of telling us something.'

'What can she tell us that we do not know?'

'Almost everything.'

There was a pause.

'Ramaz, are you trying to make me unhappy?'

'I may have often succeeded, but since when have I tried?' As there was a silence, Ramaz thought he had better continue. 'Don't forget that you are an exceptional woman, Ala.'

'Oh, you just say that.'

'Not at all. We knew each other when we were children. There was no choice in our lives – no chaos. You are from another world, the world of our villages. Our life together became a habit very early. Thamar was born into a world of incredible disorder. We do our best to keep it out, like poison gas, like pollution, but we cannot succeed completely, even on the campus. That's why we seem so ideal to a woman like Kate Dornstein. She sees a house without a television aerial, without a radio, and with a child who plays an instrument almost professionally – and she thinks of her two children. One is on a drug rehabilitation programme, and she blames everything for that, her husband, the permissive society, the American way of life. When she becomes aggressive because Thamar doesn't seem grateful enough, she is talking to her husband, flailing about her against forces she doesn't understand.'

'But I agree with her, Ramaz. Thamar does *not* seem grateful enough.'

'Why should she be grateful?'

'You can ask that?'

'And can a person not be grateful without showing it?'

'You think she is? Grateful?'

There was another pause while both stared at the ceiling for enlightenment.

'I tell you this much. We have each other. She has nobody.'

'Oh, don't start that again,' Ala moaned.

'It's a fact.'

'She has *us*.'

'We are her age?'

'We are *family*.'

'Family and friends are not the same thing. Friends are family one finds for oneself. There are things she *can't* tell us. We have to wait, and perhaps even suffer a little. In the fullness of time ...'

He kissed her, and it was clear that the conversation was at an end. He was soon snoring, and she continued to stare at the ceiling, feeling as lonely as her daughter was supposed to be. What do men know? They merely command. Perhaps it is as well that way. She sighed deeply and adopted the line of least resistance, slumber.

The next morning, at breakfast, there was not much conversation, rather was the atmosphere watchful and given to tact. Oddly, it was the usually silent Thamar who was the most garrulous.

'In six days' time I'll be 21,' she said, her mouth full of black bread and white cheese.

'We had not forgotten,' laughed the Professor. 'You know, if you keep reminding us in this way, all surprise will evaporate – and you will give us the impression we are so old there is a risk we will forget the great day.'

'All I want to say ... don't give me a present, a watch or a jewel or something – just give me the money, and let me decide ...'

'That sounds very mercenary,' murmured Ala, who believed one should be gracious rather than pragmatic at the receiving end of gifts.

'Mother, in some ways you're much younger than I am.'

'Don't talk to me like that.'

'Mother, don't you see our little girl is flattering you,' said the Professor, kissing his wife on the forehead. 'A part of you is eternally young and lovely.'

Ala smiled sadly and accepted the statement as she would have accepted a gift, with downcast eyes and apparent pleasure.

'So you want money,' said the Professor. 'Why? May I ask?'

'I'd like to give myself a present,' Thamar answered brightly.

'What?'

'If I tell you, all surprise will evaporate, to use your phrase, Papa.'

The Professor smiled one of his smiles, the lawyer's one. 'Is it possible to take yourself by surprise?'

'Oh yes. Oh yes,' cried Thamar, as though her father had fallen into a trap.

Ala looked from one to another, trying to understand. The Professor looked piercingly at his daughter, reassuringly at his wife, and announced he was late for a lecture. He then left.

Thamar finished her coffee, and hoped to go to her room before her mother found words.

'Ah, one day you will know the burden of sorrow too – when you are married in your turn ... have a family of your own ...'

Thamar ran upstairs to her room without rising to the bait. She locked the door, drew the blinds, went to a secret place among her books, withdrew a shallow box from behind some volumes of an encyclopedia, opened it with the aid of a key she

84

stored among her earrings, withdrew a fistful of money, and counted it slowly, making sure she had the amount right. She saw herself as a miser counting her hoard, and the image, direct from some old illustrated fairy story or other, gave her both strength and encouragement. Downstairs, it was in bad taste to mention money. All that counted were erudition, learned banter, Mendelssohn and the like. Upstairs, in a cranny, one could be sordid. She replaced the money and the key to the box where she had found them, and left the house in high spirits, crying out that she was going to place a long-distance call.

'A call you can make here!' said Ala to an empty entrance hall. And then added, only for her own ears, 'Who does she know?'

On the great day, Thamar teased herself by dragging out the anticipation. She came down late to breakfast.

'Ah!' cried both her parents. This was a time for kisses, for reconciliations, for great joy.

There were three presents lying on her plate, one in an envelope, one in a box, one in a floppy parcel.

'It's a good psychological test,' coaxed the Professor, after he had sung Happy Birthday to You polyphonically with his wife, making it sound like an ancient melody from the catacombs of the Caucasus. 'Let us see which she will open first!'

Thamar went for the large floppy parcel.

'Ah, ah, ah,' admonished the Professor. 'Largest is not always best!'

'In that case, it is the warmth of the heart which makes it largest,' said Ala, enigmatically.

Thamar pulled out a pinafore, embroidered by hand with motifs from northern Daghestan.

'It's for when you help me in the kitchen,' laughed Ala, as her daughter kissed her dutifully. 'Try it on, try it on.'

'Later, Mother.'

'Later, Mother,' echoed the Professor, with a plea for understanding.

Thamar undid the box. They were earrings of enormous complexity, antiques.

'They belonged to my mother, and came from Abhazia,' the Professor said. 'She gave them to me when we left for the West. When you marry and have children of your own, the first-born girl shall inherit these when she comes of age.'

'Doesn't leave much for the second-born girl,' said Thamar, as the Professor shot his wife a calculatedly expressionless look.

'They are ... wild,' Thamar added.

'Wild? Primitive, perhaps, in the way of directness of elemental strength, but wild?'

'It's an expression, like neat. Wild doesn't mean wild,' Thamar explained.

'I see,' said her father. 'What means what, I ask myself.'

'As well you may, Papa.' Thamar was hard at work on the envelope. She drew out a cheque. It was for two hundred dollars. Thamar expressed neither joy nor elation of any sort. She kissed her father. 'Thanks,' she said.

'It's what you wanted. It's only a piece of paper, with writing on it, like the Dead Sea Scrolls. Not very glamorous, for a coming of age!'

'Who wants glamour?'

'It's an important date, nevertheless.'

'You don't know just how important it is.'

'We've both been through it, your mother and I.'

'One wouldn't always know it.' She rose.

'And your breakfast?' said her mother, softly.

'Tonight we have a nice surprise for you, darling,' the Professor declared. 'Only people you like. The Helgards, with their handsome son who will be a mining engineer, the Krausses, with their daughter, Sonia. You remember Sonia Krauss? The Helgards, the Krausses, that's all. Strict intimacy. There will be stimulating conversation, a little music, only your favourite compositions, who knows, perhaps a little dancing, we could even roll up the carpet.'

'Who would play for the dancing?' asked Thamar.

'Mama can still manage a fox-trot or two, a quick-step, eh Mama?'

Ala made a gesture denoting she had forgotten everything.

'In any case, I won't be here.'

'Won't be here?' asked the Professor, incredulous. 'You are celebrating your 21st elsewhere, with other people?'

'I have already celebrated it. I'm leaving for about a week.'

'A week? Where to?'

'Boston.'

'Boston?' cried the Professor, as though she had said Beijing.

'Yes. It's a long-standing engagement.'

'How long, may one ask?'

'Oh five, six years.'

'So it isn't ...'

'I don't have to tell you who or what it is. I have come of age.'

'We are still your parents, your family,' Ala wailed, attempting unsuccessfully to make it sound reasonable.

'And who will play 'cello tonight?' asked the Professor calmly, and added, 'Mother refuses to play with me, sonatas. You are our pride, our joy.'

'Then play your unaccompanied Bach suites,' Thamar suggested casually.

'It is you they come to hear, Thamar. You are the miracle we wrought.'

'Mistakes and all?'

'You noticed?'

'Noticed? They were deliberate. Deliberate! I didn't have to make them. I decided to,' snapped Thamar with unrestrained hostility. Then she calmed down, and said quietly, 'I'm going out now, to make a long-distance call.'

'A long-distance call you can make here, if it's not too long. It's Boston, perhaps? Please ...'

But Thamar had gone.

'Deliberate?' echoed the Professor. 'The errors she didn't have to make?' He looked at his wife. She had tears trembling between her eyelids, making her eyes huge.

'And she didn't even try on her pinafore.'

For once the Professor lost his restraint. 'A pinafore? And my sacred mother's earrings, so jealously guarded against the great day? That's nothing, I suppose.' He recovered his sense of balance. 'Ala, there is something here we fail to understand.'

But it was too late for logic. Ala's large tears were falling like tropical raindrops on to the tablecloth.

The first experiments were extraordinary. Thamar looked at herself in the mirror, and felt, for the first time in her life, that it was possible for someone halfway decent to fall in love with her.

'I think I can safely say it's a pretty good job,' said Dr Brisket, standing behind her in his green hospital garb, and looking critically at his handiwork. 'I didn't make it quite as short as you had stipulated,' he went on, 'because I figured you felt that way as a reaction to the somewhat lengthy proboscis Mother Nature fixed you with —'

'Mother Nature, my foot,' Thamar interrupted. 'My parents.'

'Do they have prominent noses?' Dr Brisket asked.

'They both,' laughed Thamar. She could actually laugh about it now.

'Yes, well, I just had it turn up ever so slightly at the tip,' Dr Brisket went on, looking at her intently in the mirror, and illustrating what he was talking about by using his little finger as a pointer. 'The male animal cares for that.' He grinned. 'My experience tells me.' Then he grew serious again. 'The nostrils were the toughest part of the job, I guess. I had to remodel them completely, and hide the traces. Overly flared nostrils give a person an expression of carnality which isn't terribly attractive, I find. Balance is the most important feature in beauty, and it's often overlooked. Balance, by which I mean harmony. And I think that's what we have here. Harmony.'

'It'll take me years to get used to it.'

'Oh sure,' laughed Dr Brisket. 'You'll probably blow your nose into a handkerchief held an inch away from the tip, you'll pinch your upper lips with a fork at meal times, trying to find your mouth, and you might even have difficulties judging distances while driving.'

'I don't drive,' said Thamar.

'Don't drive? Hm. Rara Avis.'

'What?'

'There aren't many of you people left.'

'No there aren't. And I'm not one of them. No longer,' replied Thamar enigmatically.

She had begun to think of her return. It would be as brief as possible, because it was bound to be painful. She would get a job, secretarial, administrative, menial even, or perhaps playing the 'cello, anything to leave a home she had outgrown, which forced her into everlasting childhood, everlasting subservience to her father's saws and wisecracks, everlasting invitation to injure her mother's gaping sensibilities. There was nothing to explain. She wore her explanation in the dead centre of her face. It was for them to argue about between themselves, at night, among the debris of pinafores and ancient earrings, stinking of metal, and piano parts and fiddle parts, and masses of glutinous rice and nuts and raisins, the aftermath of entertainments. If need be, she would fall back on rudeness. She didn't wish to, since she was not one to cause pain gratuitously, but occasionally it was necessary, like a wrong note in a sonata, to make a point with surgical precision.

She returned home after a brief convalescence, much like a prodigal, but with one important difference. The prodigal son did not leave home ugly, and return handsome.

Her mother was the first to see her as she let herself in through the front door. Their eyes met for a brief moment. Then Ala let out a scream of such magnitude, of such penetration, that her daughter's first reaction was one of incredulity rather than of alarm. Having screamed, Ala dropped to the floor like a stone. The Professor was at home, and came scampering down the stairs. 'What have you said to her?' he asked, as he went down on his knees beside his wife.

'Not a word. I didn't have to.'

The Professor looked up at her. 'Boston? Is that where you had it done? A new nose?'

'Yes. You see, I told you I could give myself a present, and still take myself by surprise. I had no idea how it would look.'

'And the surprise was a pleasant one? That button in the middle of your face?'

'It gives me confidence.'

The Professor's dismay turned to anger. 'What's the matter, my nose, your mother's nose, weren't good enough for you? Where's your character gone? Your personality? Now you look exactly like everybody else.'

'Maybe that's what I wanted, to lose myself in the crowd!' shouted Thamar.

Their nascent quarrel came to an end when Ala stirred. 'Oh, Ramaz, have you ... have you seen our girl?' she whispered.

'I have, I have. She is alive and well.'

'A terrible accident. It must have been a drunken driver. She is disfigured.'

'No, no.'

'Disfigured, I tell you. Her nose has gone. They have tried to replace it. They have not succeeded. My joy, my flower, my life, has lost her nose.' And she began wailing inconsolably according to the ancient habits of her ancestors in their impregnable hill places, wailing and beating her breast, symbolically rather than painfully.

'Now see what you have done,' said the Professor, rising, since he was of no further use on his knees.

'What a fuss to make about a nose job,' observed Thamar, shutting the front door.

'Who cares about a nose?' the Professor said, loudly, to make himself heard through the wailing. 'It's not that which is important. It is the fact of interfering with nature. Come into my study for a moment. I want to talk to you. No, no, leave Mother on the carpet. She is happy there.' They went into the Professor's study.

'A nose in itself isn't much, skin, bone, tissue. But it is a mark, a personal trademark. We came from ancient stock, up in the mountains of the Caucasus. We breathe the pure, thin air of the upper atmosphere, we drink sour milk and eat lamb on a skewer, together with pungent herbs; it is a savage, healthy life, and a long one. According to rumour, my grandfather is still alive . somewhere above the clouds. He can still dance, climb a sheer rock face, and drink himself into a stupor with the best of them, and his nose is an organ of such massive strength, that if he charged a bull, the bull would suffer a nosebleed.'

'But Papa, you talk as if we still lived up there instead of on an American campus on the edge of a smog-ridden industrial zone. We don't, and I'd rather have a nose which is acceptable in a cosmetic-oriented society than have one able to charge a cow and cause damage. I guess it's what we want out of life. I never knew the Caucasus. I only knew New

Jersey. You can't force me to share your fantasies. I have my own.'

The Professor smiled. 'At last, you're talking. That is a victory in itself. If it's the nose which has released your tongue, good luck to them both. We will survive, even if we never quite get used to your man-made feature.'

'As opposed to God-made?'

'Precisely. You do understand.'

'When you and Mother had sex, the result was God-made?'

'Please don't be vulgar, my daughter.'

'That is the height of pretension. I had *your* nose. *Yours* and *Mother's*. It is the *same* nose. Once you two got together, there was no other possibility left open to me. God had nothing whatever to do with it!'

'Keep your ideas to yourself. They may well be shocking to some people,' murmured the Professor. 'But nature may well take its revenge on you. Mark my words. Whenever man interferes with nature, he runs a terrible risk – whether he tries to alter the course of a river or create hybrids. Nature keeps its reply for the most unexpected moments – and when we least expect it –' The Professor made a gesture of a blade falling, using one hand to fall sideways on to the palm of the other. He smiled again, almost warmly.

'But don't bother about us, and our reactions. We will survive this, as we have survived revolution, war, famine, Ellis Island, and the Turks. Perhaps you have noticed that Mother stopped wailing almost as soon as we stepped into my study. It is a tradition of the Abhazian highlands that they stop wailing once there is no one to listen to them.'

In fact, life resumed almost normally, but there were differences. When Professor Vrbicki, of the Department of Zoology, dropped round with his clarinet to play the Brahms (always a painful experience, since they had to play the Scherzo at half speed to accommodate his abilities), Thamar was sent to the movies. The Atoulias didn't want the nose to dominate every conversation, nor were they eager for dreary speculations about genetics or the right of free choice in a democratic society. Thamar was glad to go to the movies since she never had the opportunity for going anywhere, or seeing anything away from the intellectual high jinks at home. She did run into Mrs Dornstein while out shopping, and had praises poured on her nose. Mrs Dornstein was eager to have an eye shifted on to what she imagined was the level of the other eye, and had to have the address of the plastic surgeon who had done such a brilliant job. She was about as neurotic as everyone else on the campus, and keen as mustard on appearance.

'I was full of praise for your parents the other day,' she confided in Thamar in the car park of the supermarket, 'and I said you ought to be grateful, but I always recognized that living with them must be *utter hell*. I mean, they're not of this century, not of this part of the world. No car, no television, no radio even. It's a wonder they have an ice-box. Sure you can make a fire by rubbing two sticks together, but *come on* – it sure is easier by electricity. And, for what it's worth, let me tell you, they ought to have their noses fixed, both of them. These days there's no need to live with bad teeth or bad noses or bad eyes or bad anything. Just about anything can be fixed. And personally, I'd rather have a great nose than play classical fiddle.'

Thamar hardly joined in the conversation. She didn't have to. Mrs Dornstein kept the flame of dialogue fanned all by herself, by her own effort to communicate, to share, to do all those wholesome things which have driven people mad exulting in freedom as one exults in bubble baths, in drink, in drugs, in any excess. Thamar remembered Dr Brisket's insistence on harmony, on balance. It meant judgment based on both personal opinion and on opinion received, on give and take. Finally, no wholesale judgment can be right. Neither the vacillating, garrulous outpourings of Mrs Dornstein, nor the static, immovable, rules of her father, applied in the belief that people who had not moved since biblical times had no need to move today. And if the truth were told, both of them cheated. At moments Mrs Dornstein confessed herself lost, even to herself, and shed bitter tears about men in general, and her man in particular, and at times Professor Atoulia liked an iced beer of a kind and frigidity unknown within hundreds of square miles of Mount Ararat.

It was not too difficult for Thamar, presentable, discreet, and intelligent, to find a job. She aimed low to start with, becoming the cashier in a ladies' hairdressers, and fairly soon thereafter, becoming the secretary of a local real estate company. She earned enough money to leave home, although she left some old clothes and a few dishevelled dolls in her room at the request of her father, so that the parents still had the impression of an unseen, but deeply felt umbilical cord stretched over the nearby landscape. She lived in a one-room apartment built in a conventional modern style as though it could be moved at any given moment, or reduced to rubble in a matter of seconds. She acquired a portable television set, and took driving lessons. It was an extraordinary, character-forming adventure catching up with ordinary people, and at times she felt as though she had spent childhood and youth in a seminary, protected from the world and its false values by substituting values as false, but otherworldly.

Meanwhile the joy had vanished from the Atoulia household. They no longer did much entertaining, and Ala aged visibly, as though it were not a child they had lost, but a kind of prodigy, or prophet. The Professor still impressed visitors with his sagacity, but even there times were changing. Washington hardly consulted him any more. The administration changed to one at once more scientifically oriented and slapdash, more aleatory and seemingly meticulous. If these attributes seem incompatible, even incongruous and grotesque, it is because Washington is uniquely capable of parading many aspects of its complicated character at one and the same time, and pity the poor commentators whose life-work it is to make sense of it.

Be that as it may, a high-minded gesture in favour of human rights, self-determination, or whatever the current freedom-loving fad of the time was, encouraged the administration to engage in a covert military operation in Kurdistan. It was an unmitigated disaster, ending up in several helicopters being lost at sea. The name of the sea was classified information, which was just as well, since Kurdistan is nowhere remotely close to any large body of water. The expedition, under the leadership of a Major-General, evidently mistook Kurdistan for somewhere else, or rather to be more accurate, mistook somewhere else for Kurdistan, which proved, yet again, that the American talent is too brash, too hearty, too hail-fellow-ill-met for covert operations of any kind, and that the American bump for locality is, to say the least, hazy, off the beaten freeway.

To the Professor, this disaster was uniquely attributable to the fact that he had not been consulted. He cut out the reports from the *New York Times*, and other papers, and carried quite a dossier in his pocket, ready to produce it at a second's notice, and read selected passages to whoever was willing to listen. He also wrote a number of sarcastic letters to newspapers and periodicals, some of which found their way into print, but in very abbreviated form. The Professor took to carrying around the printed copies of his letters as well, together with photocopies of his originals for comparison. He began slowly to realize that he had fallen out of favour, since his expertise no longer corresponded with the needs of a new generation of administrators. All his old contacts had retired, or gone back to the more lucrative practices in the public sector.

And even on the campus, other unpleasant truths were looming. His boring old crony Professor Buke retired with a bottle or two to the American Virgin Islands, the University having decided during its economy drive that Sumerian studies were too esoteric to warrant a whole-time chair. Admittedly, Professor Atoulia's range was wider, and his grasp of it more convincing than Professor Buke's over the half-buried mysteries of Sumer, but nevertheless what had once appeared as a scholastic necessity now began to seem an extravagant luxury. The Dornsteins retired soon afterwards of their own volition, the renegade son having died of an overdose just when he seemed to be doing 'so well'.

The night was closing in. Occasional friends departed as arbitrarily as during wars, and it was too late to make new ones.

The Professor and his wife still stared at the ceiling in the darkness, but they had little to say to each other.

'How old am I?' Ala asked.

'Why ask me?'

'You know everything.'

'As usual, you exaggerate.'

Pause. A long one.

'You are three years younger than I am. I am 68. So how old are you?'

'Tell me. Please. I haven't the power to think.'

'Sixty-five.'

'And how much longer must I live?'

'I know everything?'

'Please, Ramaz.'

'Well, it's one of the features of our homeland that nobody knows their real ages. Your grandfather was supposed to be 143 when he died. But people exaggerate, especially when they have nothing else to do in life. He probably was not over 120.'

'Oh, he was.'

'All right, 125. Once you're up there, what's the difference? You're probably not 65, but 42.'

'No, no. More. More.'

'How old were you when you had Thamar?'

'Forty.'

'So, you must be 61. She's 21.'

'How old are you then?'

'Sixty-four. Here they like you to retire at 65. Unless you're Einstein. Then it's 66. Satisfied?'

There was another pause. Since there was no snoring, Ala had the courage to ask another question.

'Are you happy with your life?'

'Now you ask me – just as I'm preparing for the night?'

'What better time?'

'Well, I'll tell you then. I never thought of myself as conservative, and I still don't. Admittedly, I dealt with the past, all my life, but that doesn't make me a conservative. I know medieval values and perhaps I may be guilty of applying them. I accept what I am given, gratefully. The proof? I still have the nose which God gave me.'

'The teeth? The teeth which God gave you? Are they the ones in the glass beside your bed?'

The Professor suddenly rocked with laughter, so that the bed shook. 'For someone with no humour, you are sometimes very amusing.'

'It was not my intention,' said Ala. 'We were speaking of God and his gifts. You are a man. It is easier for a man with such a nose. If you hadn't existed, perhaps I would never have married. Then we would have no occasion to chat at night. And I would not have understood our girl, after all this time.'

'You understand her?'

'Not what she did. Only why she did it. And it makes me sad. Because of you, I never had the need to understand very much.'

'When such things are more or less arranged by families, it is easier. Oh, I know there's a lot of romantic nonsense talked, Mr Right, all that - but when it's an arrangement, you make it your business to love a specific person, and it quickly becomes a habit, and habits are much more difficult to break than romantic attachments. It's a fact. More habit, less divorce.'

'I love you when you talk like that. It makes me feel safe.'

'You are safe. We have a little liberty within our social structure, and we use it to the full. These people here, the Americans, let me tell you, they spend their time speaking of freedom as though it were something only they possess, something they invented, but they have no sense of measure. When you are thirsty, you take a drink of water. You don't have to drown in a reservoir to quench your thirst. They haven't realized that, and they probably never will. They are all prisoners in a vast prison without bars, forced into conformity by the endless barrage of publicity, hankering after the same images, the same noses —'

'The same teeth.'

'I waited for you to say that. That's habit too. Extrasensory perception. Knowing another mind. The great victory over solitude.'

'Thank you for talking to me like that. It's like looking at a wonderful book, full of pictures. Now, go to sleep.'

'I could see that coming too. You excite me into eloquence, and when I am fully awake, you invite me to fall asleep.' Both were smiling in the dark, but neither saw the other.

At about the time of the Professor's retirement,

Thamar first met Bruce Connahy. Both events were important. Financial considerations forced the Atoulias to move right away from the vicinity of the University, and take up residence in a large block of dingy apartments, with fire-escapes and other appendages cascading down its outer walls, and a huge fading telephone number on its wall (it had been changed since). It was two blocks from the sea-front in a city renowned for gambling and sleazy pastimes, and like all such places, it frequently screamed of solitude, of man's isolation in a crowd of human indifference. They could not take Ala's grand piano with them, since there was no room for it, and the Professor could not even play his violin very softly, since next door lived an old lady with a venerable terrier for companionship. This ancient bitch howled every time it heard the fiddle, although it slept peacefully to the sound of the vacuum-cleaner. As the Professor said philosophically, 'There is no accounting for tastes.'

Their chosen mode of life became more and more difficult. It is one thing to isolate yourself on a university campus, which is by definition removed from reality and rarefied. It is quite different to do so in an apartment with thin walls, with hundreds of other people slotted into the honeycomb, their fate forced on them by a lack of money and an end of prospects.

'This is freedom?' asked the Professor rhetorically.

He still had cards made announcing his change of address, and sent them to many of his old contacts and quite a few authorities within the State Department in case the Kurdish fiasco should have opened the administration's eyes to the evident truth about its shortcomings. The Professor received one or two acknowledgments, but no invitations to a resumption of activity. Even the several magazines he used to write for, such as *Khyber Gazette* and *Kurdish Newsletter*, the one published in Duluth, the other in Beaumont, Texas, explained that times were exceptionally hard.

'Knowledge used to be at a premium,' the Professor told his wife, 'but now we are all swimmers in a vast ocean of mediocrity. Of what use is the judgment I have acquired over the years, balancing this fact against that, using my mastery of Georgian, Armenian, Turkish, Kurdish, Persian, and a host of local dialects? None at all. It is like valuable furniture rotting in a depository. What is there to talk about in this hostile environment? I found a couple of Iranians serving in the shopping mall, but they are base characters who will do well in America because they understand the rules without difficulty, and because they have no qualifications to tie them to disciplines, and eventually, to regrets. There is an old Kurd too, who takes money for deckchairs down by the sea, but he doesn't speak a word of Kurdish, or perhaps he just refuses to. Keeps saying he's a good American as though someone had accused him of being a bad one. Told me with a cackle, one thing they don't have in Kurdistan is television. That, in itself, is apparently reason enough to be a good American.'

Out of cussedness, and perhaps because conversation was losing its attraction, Ala becoming more and more silent in bewilderment at this hermetic existence in a box, Ramaz invested in a small television set for the first time in his life, and he and his wife, thus relieved of the need for contact, sat and watched inane parlour games, with questions, to which he shouted out the answers long before the panel contestants got it wrong, or else episodes of a series running at that time called 'Knoxville', a saga of family greed, vainglory, avarice, and murder presented as a model to all lone rangers in a land of opportunity. Ala's particular favourite quickly became 'Ultradame', a science-fiction tale of a massive female in a cellophane bikini, who chased the bad guys into outer space, and confounded their plans for world domination, whatever that might mean. The fact that they had only one small black-and-white set between them now created new difficulties, as one was always biding one's time, looking at something without interest while waiting more or less eagerly for something more congenial to turn up.

Thamar used to call every now and then for a chat, but there was an aura of duty about it which took away the pleasure from the old people. She had moved even further away into a larger inland city, where she was now the so-called Girl Friday of an attorney, and doing exceptionally well. And then, there was Bruce Connahy. Bruce, a fairly tall, fairly heavy young man with a blonde crew cut, which, added to his inherent courtesy and consideration, gave him a distinctly old-fashioned presence. He can't be said to have courted Thamar. He was just always there, slipping into his role as a consort as easily, as gracefully as he slipped into conversation or into silence, whichever was called for at the moment. Thamar began to rely on him, and he seemed utterly unsurprised by developments. Both began to regard their attachment to one another as the most natural thing in the world, and think of their youth as merely the preparation for this state of affairs.

When she was away from him, at work, Thamar tried to analyse her attraction, but was quite unable to. He was not what she could consider her type. She had no type. In fact, sexual speculations never really occupied her mind at all. Before her plastic surgery, she had trained herself to do without such luxuries, and the abandonment of that discipline had not yet burst on her with the blinding brightness of a revelation. There were too many other aspects of her independence to be savoured at the same time. But she certainly could imagine no other young man in Bruce's place. She even let him kiss her on porches, and even, sometimes, in rooms. She noticed that it was a pleasant experience, and that her breath came faster afterwards, but apart from that, it seemed a normal and momentary extension of ordinary, daily, social intercourse. The only moment of embarrassment she remembered up to now was a particularly tender farewell, when he had kissed her nose. 'I love your nose,' he had said. 'It's cute.' She had felt herself blushing. She stood on tiptoe, dragged his head down to her level, and pecked him on the nose. 'And I love yours,' she had said. 'That makes us even.'

By profession, Bruce was a chartered accountant, but his interests were many and various. He had entertained a career as a football player, which was not difficult to credit in view of his build, but his turn of speed was just inadequate for professional purposes, and left him too often at the bottom of a pile of humanity, which even the bolstering and padding could not render tolerable. He had been in the army for a while, but an inherent, and even militant docility made the more flagrant excesses of military life, such as the shouting of silly jingles in unison while cantering through an inoffensive landscape, distinctly unattractive. Gentleness was the hallmark of his nature, despite his considerable physical strength, and it was this gentleness which led to the inevitable maturing of their relationship, and a sense of fulfilment, of well-being.

They began living together when they were tired of saying goodbye, and it was the very best of reasons. Then, one day, Thamar noticed a change in herself, and went off in her lunch break to see Dr Swallbeck, a local practitioner. This bald and sentimental man was a past expert in the diffusion of good news, and he told her, with a tremolo of delight in his voice,

'Well, Mrs ... Mrs ...?'

'Connahy,' replied Thamar, without thinking.

'Mrs Connahy, there are to be three of you, for the time being.'

That evening, Thamar told Bruce that she was expecting a child. He kissed her nose warmly, went to the ice-box, poured two glasses of milk, and they toasted their good fortune.

'My parents are dead, the both of them,' said Bruce. 'It's a damn shame they couldn't have lived to see this.'

'Both dead? You never told me.'

'It's not a thing one readily talks about,' Bruce replied. 'They were separated. That is, divorced really. Dad was killed in Korea. I hardly knew him. Colonel. Lieutenant-Colonel. At least, Major, but they promoted him posthumously. Mother married again, a son-of-a-bitch called Steinhager. Drank. Ran his car off the road on Christmas Eve, killed my mom. He's married again. Lives in Florida. In the Keys.'

Thamar had never doubted his word before. She had never had occasion to. But now, for some reason, she didn't really believe him. Not that it mattered very much, except that she didn't like not believing him. She'd rather believe him all the time, even about things that didn't really matter.

'I still have my parents,' she said, and then added, as a precaution, remembering the noses, 'but of course, my mother isn't my real mother.'

'Oh?'

'No. Papa married his first cousin when my real mother passed away. But we all pretend she is my real mother – it's a kind of family pact.'

'Sure, I understand.'

'The only trouble is, of course, we don't look terribly alike. My own mother – I hardly knew her, but I've seen photographs – she was very attractive. She was ... an actress ... back in the old country. But when she came over here, there was the language barrier, you know.'

'Sure. It's a little tough for us to imagine, but I guess I do know. I'd like to meet your folks. Your present folks, that is. I mean, your dad and ... what you explained to me.'

'You will, in the fullness of time,' she said, borrowing a phrase from her father.

At the earliest opportunity, she travelled to visit her parents. She had never visited them since they moved, and she experienced a little difficulty finding the address.

She was appalled at the poky apartment after the pleasant house where she had grown up, but hoped that she had masked her feelings convincingly. Her mother shed copious tears on seeing her again, and even wailed a little until the aged terrier picked up her cue from next door, and joined in the jubilation. The Professor did his best to appear rational and busy. 'I still write the occasional article,' he said, 'and the administration rang only the other day to ask for some advice.'

'But where is the Steinway?' asked Thamar.

'A Steinway? Through that door? Up those stairs? Are you joking?'

'You sold it? And what's that? A television? You?'

'It's only a small one, as you can see. Therefore it's only a small concession. A small breach of principle.'

'And the violin?'

'It irritates Her Majesty the Fox Terrier next door. You heard her just now when mother was wailing. For Johann Sebastian Bach, it's twice as bad.'

'But that's *terrible*.'

The Professor brought his fist down on a table. He spat out the words. 'We have survived! We are survivors, your mother and I. We roll with the punch, as they say, but we're always back again, like ninepins, waiting for the next catastrophe. That's us!'

It was when he was determined and outspoken that Thamar noticed how her father had aged. Effort underlines the sum of years.

'Tell us about yourself,' said Ala, now that Ramaz had had his say. She gathered Thamar's hands into her own, and sat gazing at her like a fortune-teller without inspiration.

'I live. I live quite well.'

'You are with a hairdressing organization?' asked her father.

'No. That was long ago. I'm the right hand ... the assistant of a lawyer.'

'A lawyer.' The Professor brightened visibly. 'International?'

'Corporate.'

'And no sign of a good man?' asked Ala.

'Yes ... yes ...' responded Thamar quietly.

'Aha, aha, aha!' broke in the Professor, with comic eagerness. 'Someone from our part of the world, by good fortune?'

'No.'

The Professor had a moment of fear. 'But ... Christian?'

'Yes.'

'Praise to the Lord on high.'

Ala nodded sadly, as though sadness was the greatest of satisfactions.

'Well, don't leave us in suspense!' snapped the Professor.

'His name is Bruce. Bruce Connahy.'

'Connahy? What kind of name is that?'

'Irish.'

'Irish? You hear that, mother?'

'I hear that,' intoned Ala, miserably.

'And when may we meet him?'

'One day. Soon.'

'Is it not important that we approve of him?' asked Ala.

'Of course, but I'm sure you'll like him.'

'What does he do in life?' demanded the Professor.

'He's a chartered accountant.'

The Professor nodded. 'I could have hoped for better. I could have feared for worse.'

'And some time, after we meet him, you hope to marry?' Ala said.

'Perhaps even before that,' replied Thamar. 'You see, I'm expecting.'

Ala clapped her hands together fatalistically, and began moaning.

'For God's sake, Mother, think of the dog,' hissed the Professor. 'Things are done differently these days. All topsy-turvy, if that is the correct phrase. People have children, and then decide to marry, or not, as though the children were not there. Does he still wish to marry you despite your pregnancy?'

'Of course. What do you take him for?'

'Praise to God. Hosannah.'

'What do you take him for?' Thamar insisted. 'You have not yet given us the opportunity of judging for ourselves.'

'And that should make a difference to *my choice*?'

There was an awkward silence in the room.

'There's another thing,' said Thamar, at length. 'I expect your help in the matter.'

'And what is it?' the Professor asked, with some misgiving.

'It's because of my altering the shape of my nose.'

'I knew no good would come of it,' Ala said, most of her handkerchief in her mouth.

Thamar turned on her mother. 'If I'm a happy, balanced creature today, it's because I did what I did. I have no regrets, you understand. No regrets. Not one! But obviously,' – and she continued more reasonably – 'if Bruce meets the two of you, with your identical noses, he'll know in a trice that I've had mine fixed, and *there is no need for him to know*! I refuse to let him know! So ...'

'So, what's the solution?' asked the Professor.

'So I've told him that Mother's not my real mother.'

'What?' shouted the Professor. 'How can you be so inhuman. If you must tell lies, tell him that I'm not your real father, but never, for God's sake, say that your mother is not your real mother!'

'I have already told him. I can't change my story now!' Thamar shouted back. 'I said my real mother died, and you married your first cousin. How else d'you expect Bruce to accept that you look so like each other, and I look so different from either? If you want to meet Bruce, and to see the child, you'd better stick with my story.'

'The devil take you and your child,' yelled the Professor. 'Never come back here. Leave us with our personal tragedy. Go away from here to your life of vice. We are childless. Better be childless than do what you have done. Go away. Leave us. Don't even say goodbye. Don't bother!'

Ala dropped to the floor and tried to caress Thamar's legs while the Professor indulged his transport of passion. Thamar dragged her mother to the front door as gently as possible, while the neighbours hammered at the wall, and the terrier made its contribution.

Several days later, a large colour television set arrived with a printed card dedicated to wonderful parents. It was Thamar's peace offering. At first, the

Professor refused to have anything to do with it. Then his curiosity overcame him, and he settled to watch an episode of 'Knoxville' in exquisite colour. To Ala he remarked during a quiet moment of chicanery on the screen, 'Our daughter, she must be earning well to afford such presents.'

'It could be the Irishman,' Ala said morosely. 'He could be wealthy.'

Thamar thought it a little strange that Bruce had changed the phone number twice, and insisted it be unlisted. It served her purposes quite well to disappear as much as possible, so she didn't think overmuch about it, but nevertheless, she registered the fact in her little hoard of mysteries. His behaviour, on the other hand, could only be described as exquisite. He made it seem as though both of them were pregnant, that it was a shared experience. Naturally he asked about her visit to her parents, and expressed his eagerness to meet them.

'Oh,' sighed Thamar, 'you have your drama, I have mine.'

'Christ,' said Bruce, 'nothing real bad I hope.'

'Mother, that is, the lady I call Mother, she's gotten a lot worse. It's a kind of senility I guess. She believes she's my real mother – acts that way, with a lot of tears, grabbing, a kind of animal possessiveness, know what I mean?'

'I can imagine. How about your dad?'

'Oh, he goes along with it. I think he thinks he's

humouring her but it's not the right way to go about it. You got to be tough, otherwise they get what they want, which is you, body and soul. I been through it all, from birth. Sure I'm caring, but by mail, by phone, I'm caring long-distance.'

'Maybe if I talked to them . . .'

Thamar took refuge in the mystique of maternity. 'Bruce, I'd rather not even talk about it until after I've given birth. I felt for a moment like I was going to lose the baby while I was with them.'

'Oh, no.'

'I did too. Once it's over, then we'll be good and kind to everybody, your people and mine.'

'My people are dead.'

'I'm sorry I mentioned it, Bruce. My people.'

They married in a simple civil ceremony, and felt much relieved. They celebrated in a snack-bar. Under Bruce's insistence, Thamar gave up her job when her pregnancy became noticeable. The lawyer offered to keep it open for her, but Bruce came home one day in a state of great excitement.

'Honey,' he cried, 'we're moving!'

'Now, just when I need to feel settled, and close to Dr Swallbeck?'

'I'm sorry about that, but this is important. We're moving right away, not just locally. I got a job in La Jolla, California!' and he let out a football shriek, a rodeo shriek, of enthusiasm. 'Palm trees, the ocean, the sun! Ideal conditions for a healthy childhood! Isn't that *wonderful!*'

Thamar had to admit that, as a prospect, it made

mincemeat of Dr Swallbeck, and other neighbour-
hood considerations. After all, had her family not
given birth for generations on rocky crags quite
unsuitable for the purpose, only assisted by a passing
goatherd, a total stranger? And was it not safer to be
separated from her folks by a whole expansive
continent than by a shuttle on a local feeder line? She
quickly shared his excitement, and prepared for the
move while he spent the last days at the office.

It was on the eve of their departure, at about the
hour Bruce usually came home, that the phone rang.
It had not done so at all since the last change of
number, so Thamar picked it up with a trace of
misgiving. 'Hello,' she said.

'Hi,' replied a pleasant enough man's voice. 'Is
Bruce there?'

'Bruce? He's not home yet. Who is this?'

'Tim.'

'Tim?'

'His brother. Who are you?'

'Me, I'm his wife, Mrs Connahy.'

'Don't be ridiculous, he wouldn't do a thing like
that without telling us.'

'Us?'

'His parents and me.'

'His parents? But they're ... I was told they'd
passed away.'

Just then Bruce came in. He was alarmed when he
saw his wife on the phone. 'Who is it?'

'Your brother? Tim?' From then on, she only
heard one side of the conversation.

'Hello, Tim? ... That's my business, I told you not to phone, not to even try ... What if it is? Does that make it your business, or anyone else's but mine? ... How did you find this number anyhows ... If you turn up here, I'll sock you, I mean it ... I don't care if we are the same size ... You can tell them whatever the hell you like ... Tell them she's black or yellow or red or any goddam colour ... You can tell them we got kids if you like ...' And then he calmed down. 'Look Tim, there's only one truth and I got it right here, and man, I'm happy ... Yeah, well it's my life, mine and hers and whatever may follow ... O.K., O.K., I'll meet you, but on neutral ground, not here, or there ... I'll meet you at eight tomorrow night, at Delaney's Bar ... That's right, in New Orange ... Then we'll talk, right? ... Right? Only till then, don't try to phone back, or I'll sock you when I see you, right? ... And cut out the crap about being my brother ... I don't care who you think you are ... Brotherly love, my ass ... O.K.?' And he hung up.

Thamar looked at him, at once piercingly and defensively. 'You won't be here at eight o'clock tomorrow evening.'

Bruce kissed her nose. 'I know that, but he don't. We'll be in Ca-lie-forn-eye-eh!'

'Is he really your brother?'

'Na-ah. He's the son of that guy in Florida I told you about.'

'But he seemed to say your parents are still alive.'

'*His* parents are still alive. Sure. He always wants

119

me to consider them as *my* parents, but they're not. I guess he wants a brother badly. I don't.'

'But they seem to live locally.'

'Key Biscayne, Florida, last I heard. But, of course, they may have moved. I don't make it my business to know.'

The answers all sounded glib enough, and uttered without reflection, for Thamar to accept them as true, although for some reason she was always expecting Bruce to make a mistake. Also Tim's voice had sounded innocent and even charming, not unlike Bruce's own.

The next morning they moved to California, and by early evening, a time at which Tim had no doubt given up on his recalcitrant brother, or else was leaning loaded on the bar, the last of Delaney's customers, Bruce and Thamar were on their balcony. They could just see the sea over the roof-tops and through the forest of television aerials, but with their eyes shut, it felt like heaven. Dr Swallbeck was replaced by a Dr Kattawalla, the next morning, an Indian gynaecologist with the manners of a guru, who crooned ancient platitudes as though he held the secret to the meaning of life. Thamar was used to this Asiatic tendency and she felt quite at home in this insinuating mist of joss-sticks and raga music through which Dr Kattawalla dispensed his instructions, his mouth cracking words as though they were nuts, but always softly.

Bruce was evidently happy in his new job, and the time of childbirth approached in a serenity in which both Tim and the Atoulias seemed memories of a grimmer world. Thamar bought a small Japanese car and a small Japanese dog as a preparation for responsibility. The dog bounced rather than sprang from the car seats to floor, from sofa to carpet and back again, and had to be watched all the time, albeit with merriment and good humour as it methodically tried to destroy things much larger than itself. Eventually, it had to be taken to a kennel for a week while Thamar was in hospital actually being delivered of her child.

Dr Kattawalla turned out to be a mixture between a seer and an athletics coach, thereby satisfying Thamar's nostalgia for both a paternal and a conjugal presence during those difficult half-conscious moments.

'Now push for all you're worth!' Dr Kattawalla suddenly instructed. Then, half-withdrew what he had said. 'Be aware of your child's wishes. Do not compel it to any rash action. Put yourself in her shoes, or rather, bare feet.'

'Hers ... hers ...?'

'Oh yes, it's a girl all right, I can see nothing to disprove it. Now concentrate. Allow nothing to deflect your single-mindedness. One. Two. Don't rush it. Three! Push with all your might! Have you ever seen an elephant moving logs? You are as powerful as that at this moment. There! What did I tell you? You have brought a beautiful young lady into the world!'

They decided to call her Ala Muriel, after the two

absent mothers, and took a great many pictures with a Polaroid camera. For her parents, Thamar dressed up in the pinafore and the grandmother's earrings as soon as she was able, holding the baby in the one hand and the dog in the other. They attempted to give as full an impression as possible of their life together, believing that such evidence of happiness could hardly fail to find an echo in the minds of the Professor and his wife. Nevertheless, they waited until Bruce had to go down to San Diego on business before mailing them.

'San Diego,' said the Professor, looking at the postmark through a magnifying glass which he now wore round his neck on a cord in order to look at the fine print wherever it turned up. His wife merely nodded, and made little whimpering noises of comprehension. She had largely given up talking as a useless occupation, especially since she shared her life, what there was of it, with someone who derived a physical pleasure from talking, someone for whom talking was tantamount to exercise. In fact, they only rarely left their apartment, the Professor only to buy rice, raisins and other condiments at the supermarket, which enabled him to exchange a few cultural words with the Iranian lads, who were rapidly forgetting their mother tongue as they learned a functional form of basic English. He would occasionally brave the ocean-front in order, as he said, to blow the cobwebs away. Ala didn't go out at

all, but just sat and stared at television, whatever
was on. The nature of the programme didn't seem to
register, and the unctuous preacher with his for-
mula for instant heaven or the busybody female
psychiatrist with her snap answers to everybody's
problems rated the same fixed stare and slightly
twisted smile.

'San Diego,' repeated the Professor, 'but still no
address. And yet a lot of goodwill, of consideration.
Pictures of the baby. I told you they named her Ala,
after you.'

Ala brushed the information aside as though
protecting food from flies, and produced a few
denigrating squeaks.

'It's nice. I find it nice. And there are my earrings.
And your pinafore,' said the Professor, holding the
magnifying glass over the pictures for Ala to see. She
did so obediently, and gurgled with what may well
have passed for pleasure.

'Yes, it's nice, all that,' said the Professor, more
darkly. 'But I tell you something – something they
will never know – something they will never have
occasion to find out. I'm *glad* I don't know where they
are – what street, what number, what telephone in
San Diego. I will never forgive Thamar for what she
did to you. Never.'

Ala covered her eyes with her hand, and shook her
head listlessly from side to side.

'After all, she's a woman. Certainly *now* she's a
woman, and for a woman to be so heartless to deny
to another woman, her mother yet, the fact of

motherhood, is one of the most horrible acts it is possible to perpetrate in this world of shadows.'

By now Ala was sobbing, and threatening to moan. It was almost as though the Professor was starved of reactions to what he had to say, and therefore endlessly rekindled dying embers in order to have some palpable satisfaction out of his diatribes, some result.

'And all this tragedy, this disruption of family feeling, of elementary tenderness, of piety towards parents, of love and respect should be due to something as paltry, as insignificant, as derisory as a *nose*, is the final insult, the ultimate slap in the face, the victory of cacophony over the harmony we produced when we surrendered our sensibilities for a few hours to Mendelssohn, Dvořak, and Beethoven. Cacophony! Cymbalum Mundi. The chorus of demons.'

Ala had taken to pulling out handfuls of her hair as an alternative means of expressing her anguish, one which did not disturb the bitch next door. Now the Professor had to struggle with her in order to curb her enthusiasm, which wasn't easy. He managed to seize her wrists, but she fought with surprising vigour.

'Are you quite mad?' the Professor panted. 'One can't even talk with you any more these days. You wish to be bald?' When she had calmed down, which was less due to anything the Professor had said, but rather to the fact that he switched on the television, he announced grimly and with determination, 'I have only one more word to say on the subject, and then I will be silent for ever. Whatever revenge, whatever retribution there is, it will be terrible.'

There was no reaction from Ala this time, since she was staring at a commercial for a personal deodorant.

Life in La Jolla was almost ideal. Thamar took up tennis, and seemed to have a real aptitude for it. She played twice a week, the pram by the side of the court, the dog sitting by the axle of the pram, to which it was tied, and gazing in perplexity at the course of the ball through a mass of hair. She regained her figure and looked after all of her charges with application while Bruce won promotion in his firm. They were the ideal young couple who understood the possibilities of a society people never ceased to cover with adulation, but which some of them either abused, or else failed to take advantage of, either through lack of modernity in their outlook, or else through a desire to have too much too quickly, to be a success in a success-oriented marketplace.

There was only one small cloud in an otherwise cloudless sky. One day, when Thamar was laying out one of Bruce's suits to be delivered to the dry-cleaner, she emptied his pockets at the moment he wandered into the room in his underwear, looking for something to put on.

'I want to empty my own pockets,' he said.

'I've always done them for you,' she replied. 'You've never raised any objection.'

'I know that,' he said, 'and I have absolutely no reason for it. I'd just feel happier emptying them myself.'

'O.K.' Thamar was mystified, and a little hurt.

'There! You have my wallet in your hand right now!'

'What of it? I never look into it, let alone take anything out.'

'I know that.' Bruce was conciliatory. 'I know you don't. And I have nothing to hide,' he said, with bright innocence. 'Forget it. Just forget it.'

'In future, I'll tell you when it's time for your suits to go to the cleaners. Then you can make your own arrangements,' Thamar said stiffly.

'Oh Christ,' Bruce muttered. 'I'm sorry I ever brought it up.'

It made no difference to the felicity of their daily lives, or to the warmth of their relationship, but it was nevertheless a little comma registered on the blank sheet of memory, on the debit side.

Two years passed happily and uneventfully, until just after little Ala's second birthday party, a happy and joyous event with quite a few children of new-found friends. One day, Thamar went up to little Ala's room, thinking Bruce was at his office, to find him up with his daughter, staring at her in a fixed and slightly uncanny way.

'Oh God, you gave me a shock. I didn't hear you

come in. I thought you were some intruder,' said Thamar.

'Never heard me come in? I never been out. I been here all the time.'

'Why? What are you doing up here? Aren't you needed at the office?'

'Oh sure I'm needed at the office.' Bruce seemed strangely disturbed. 'I came up here to look at my daughter.'

Even little Ala seemed somewhat subdued, and puzzled by her father's behaviour. She kept handing him toys which he either pretended he didn't see, or else took, only to hand them straight back.

'Well,' asked Thamar, 'now you've looked at her, what conclusions have you come to?'

'She's changed ...'

'She's grown, but I believe that was only to be expected.'

'Come over here.'

Little Ala was banging a teddy bear mercilessly into the ground.

'Well?'

'Her profile.'

Thamar suddenly felt a surge of blood into her head. She had, of course, noticed that the snub nose of babyhood was losing its innocence, and that personality was beginning to mould it to its own requirements, but surely it was too early to discern a manifestation of the family curse – a lot could still happen ... couldn't it?

'What about her profile?' Thamar asked bravely.

'Her nose. It's beginning to change shape. It's not going to be like either yours or mine,' Bruce said too quietly for comfort.

'How can you tell that yet?'

An undefinable tension developed in the house. Every time Bruce played with his daughter, Thamar was conscious of what he was searching for, and she began to feel a latent panic, and, at the same time, a sentiment of disbelief that Bruce should have been so abnormally perspicacious in a matter which is of minor concern to the majority of people.

As the weeks passed, nothing happened to alleviate the menace which suddenly, indefinably, hung over the household. Little Ala played away, and grew apace, oblivious to the fuss she had been causing. Her nose grew as she did, and she began to acquire a baleful expression she had not had before, as her eyes squinted pleasurably or widened in surprise over a nose the tip of which threatened to dip over the line of the mouth, giving her a slight look of malevolence in repose. It may have been her imagination, but Thamar fancied she noticed something odd in the inflections of people who leaned over her cot, and said 'She's beau-tiful.' Thamar preferred to show her off when she was asleep. Somehow, when the eyes were shut, less attention was focused on the nose, since peace of that kind is not only without personality, but, in babies, almost religious in its pristine composure.

Day by day, Thamar's feelings of guilt grew into a real and permanent problem. Once her own nose had been docked, she never realized that nature would take so little account of the fact, and that those genes responsible would revert to type in such a galling way. Bruce too revealed an instability of character he had never demonstrated before. They had little rows about nothing at all, they said things they didn't really mean, and then they said things they did really mean but shouldn't, and then everything suddenly seemed to be tarnished irretrievably. The child noticed a deterioration in the atmosphere, and became fractious, which only enhanced the premature maturity of its features. The dog was not insensitive either, and bit little Ala in a moment of mutual mistrust. Bruce talked of having the dog destroyed. 'Over my dead body,' snapped Thamar. And there were silences which lasted for hours.

Thamar was reduced to calling her father just in order to hear a friendly voice.

'You, I don't want to talk to. After what you did to your mother, never again, I said, do I wish to talk to you. And that's final. And let me tell you, before I remain silent for ever, one more thing. To drive your mother into what amounts to madness and me to the state I'm in because of the shape of a *nose* is just about the most stupid, the most degrading reason one could think of. All the great classical heroes, Oedipus, Hamlet, they did things for a reason, but never for the shape of a *nose*. Cyrano de Bergerac, he even capitalized on it. He didn't *complain*! And while I'm still on speaking terms, thanks for the television. It works perfectly. We spend all our time since your visit looking at the most cretinous rubbish ever invented by man, brought to us by man's equally remarkable technical mastery. The rest, as Hamlet declared, or someone from his entourage, I forget, is silence.' And so saying, he hung up.

Desperate, Thamar called Dr Brisket in Boston.

'How curious that you should call, Mrs Connahy ... No, no, I know what it's about. Funnily enough, I already had Mr Connahy on the line this morning.'

'You had my husband on the line?' asked Thamar in disbelief. 'I didn't know you —'

'It's probably not entirely ethical to tell you the drift of our conversation, Mrs Connahy, but since both of you obviously only called me after both of you had reached a decision, I feel I can only repeat what I told him. We never, on principle, perform aesthetic surgery on children, let alone babies. The nose must reach its final shape before we can safely tamper with it. So if I'm still in practice in twenty years' time, I'll be glad to see the young lady at that time. Thank you for your call.'

Thamar was stunned. Obviously nothing was left but honesty. But how had Bruce found out about Dr Brisket?

Over a silent dinner, Thamar suddenly said, 'Dr Brisket.'

Bruce dropped his fork with a clatter. 'What about him?'

'I called him today.'

'So?'

'So did you.'

'How do you know?'

'He told me.'

'He shouldn't have.'

'Why not?'

'Medical ethics.'

'Medical ethics?'

'That's what I said. Medical ethics.'

Thamar frowned. 'Bruce, how did you find out about Dr Brisket?'

Bruce could hardly believe his ears. 'How did I find out about Dr Brisket?'

'Bruce, this is going to be difficult for me. Please bear with me and be patient. But I've been living a lie, a dreadful lie, a foolish lie.' She was speaking with the greatest difficulty, but also with the greatest clarity. 'My parents are my real parents. My mother is my real mother. They come from the Caucasus.'

'I knew that.'

'Please don't interrupt. The Caucasus is a part of the world where there are some pretty large noses.'

Bruce began to laugh, at first silently.

'Please, Bruce ... both my people had ... or rather, have, these noses ... so you can imagine that at one time ... so did I ...'

Bruce's laughter became almost hysterical. There were tears in his eyes.

'What I'm trying to tell you, Bruce ... if you will please stop laughing ...' and she shouted 'is that I had a nose job ... the nose you see is not my own!' She began to laugh under the impulsion of Bruce's hysteria. Then, trying to kill her laughter, she yelled, 'Did you hear what I said? The nose on my face is not the nose I was born with! I had ... Bruce, please ...! I had plastic surgery ... Dr —'

'Brisket,' they called out in unison.

'Honey, get ... get my ... my jacket,' Bruce called out, hardly able to express himself, so physically exhausting had the laughter become. 'Take out ... wallet ...'

'But you never allow me to touch —'

'Take it out ... Go on ... Open it ... In there ... there's a leather ... a leather ... oh God ... a kind of ... leather folder with ph ... graphs ...'

'It's little Ala and me. You carry us with you?' She was touched, although she was laughing now, at him laughing.

'Turn ... over ...' He made wild gestures. She turned it over. There was a photo of two identical G.I.s, both with long, thin medieval noses.

'Who are they?'

'Me and my twin brother, Tim.'

'Tim is your *twin*?'

Bruce nodded, and his tears flew all over the place. 'Open it up.'

Thamar did so, to reveal an elderly couple with two young men in football attire. 'Dr and Mrs Aidan Connahy with their twin sons!' All four of them had the thin pointed noses of certain birds.

Bruce's face was contorted with effort. His face

was bathed in perspiration. He was panting for breath.

Thamar stared at him in disbelief.

'You mean that you too ...?'

'Dr Brisket,' he choked.

She now began to laugh as loudly, as mirthlessly as he, and he tried to keep up with her although he had no laughter left in him.

Upstairs, little Ala, hearing her parents' sustained outburst, parodied it by laughing as loudly, and even less enjoyably than they. Ha ha ha ha. She was not yet old enough to know what she was laughing at.